EIGHT
TIMES UP

JOHN CORR

EIGHT TIMES UP

ORCA BOOK PUBLISHERS

Library and Archives Canada Cataloguing in Publication
Corr, John, 1977–, author
Eight times up / John Corr.

Issued in print and electronic formats.
ISBN 978-1-4598-1861-3 (softcover).—ISBN 978-1-4598-1862-0 (PDF).—
ISBN 978-1-4598-1863-7 (EPUB)

I. Title.
PS8605.O768E44 2019   JC813'.6   C2018-904702-X
C2018-904703-8

Library of Congress Control Number: 2018954085
Simultaneously published in Canada and the United States in 2019

Summary: In this middle-grade novel, Riley's dad signs him up for aikido to help him manage his anxiety.

Orca Book Publishers is dedicated to preserving the environment and has printed this book on Forest Stewardship Council® certified paper.

Orca Book Publishers gratefully acknowledges the support for its publishing programs provided by the following agencies: the Government of Canada, the Canada Council for the Arts and the Province of British Columbia through the BC Arts Council and the Book Publishing Tax Credit.

Edited by Tanya Trafford
Cover design by Teresa Bubela
Cover image by Steven P. Hughes Illustration
Author photo by Maria Patrinelli

ORCA BOOK PUBLISHERS
orcabook.com

Printed and bound in Canada.

20 19 18 17 • 4 3 2 1

To my boys. You always put the ki—
and the "kid"—in aikido.

ONE

The first thing that hit me was the sound.

Screaming and banging from the kids who were already inside.

I stood in the hallway, just outside the dojo.

The thought of being tossed in with those rough kids made my stomach drop, flop and twist. It felt more like being thrown out of a plane than walking into my first aikido class.

The second thing to hit me was the smell.

I leaned a little closer, poked my nose through the doorway and sniffed. Sweet and funky at the same time. Like old gym socks.

"Go on, Riley," Dad said. "It's going to be fun!" He chopped at my neck. "Hi-YA!"

"Really, Dad?" I smacked his hand away. "A karate chop? This isn't even karate!"

My dad laughed. "C'mon, Riley, please give it a chance. I really think this will be good for you." He pulled his bag strap up on his shoulder and started down the hall. "I have some marking to do. I'll be on one of those couches in the lobby." He smiled and disappeared around the corner. I could hear his footsteps echoing.

I rubbed my neck where he had chopped me. Who knows? Maybe they *did* do karate chops in aikido.

Aikido chops?

I inched back up to the open door. I told myself that all I had to do was step through.

One step.

The voices got louder.

My heart pounded harder. My palms and back were suddenly sweaty. My eyes filled with water, making the puke-green mats swim a little. It was the start of a feeling that Mom had called "the Surge." Her hands had opened up wide when she described it. "It's when all your feelings rush up like one big tidal wave," she'd said.

"Surge is right. But for me it's not like a wave," I'd told her. "It's more like a burst of electricity hitting a robot, making all his springs pop loose and his eyes light up and his head spin around."

She'd laughed and then hugged me. She said that when her feelings rushed in like a wave, I could be her anchor. And when my feelings electrocuted me, she would be whatever it was that helped exploding robots.

That was before she left. Before her feelings surged up and carried her away. In her letter she tried to explain how bad it was when the Surge mixed with a whole other feeling called "the Shadow." She said she had some ideas about how to get better, but she didn't say what they were. Or when she'd be back.

Or *if* she'd be back.

It had only been a few weeks, but it felt like forever. The Surge had been hitting me a lot more since she left.

Dad didn't really get it. He called my feelings "anxiety." When Mom left he'd done what professors always do. He dragged me to the library.

One book said that exercise could help anxious kids calm down. That night at dinner he'd read it out loud to me. "*Physical activities such as aikido or yoga are especially good for easing a troubled young mind.*" He stopped to wipe taco crumbs off his face. "*The traditional Japanese martial art of aikido, in particular, builds cooperation skills and confidence.*"

I'd put on my best professor voice. "Well, I, in particular, do not care what that book says."

My dad used a bit of taco shell to scrape up a blob of salsa from the table. "The book says aikido or yoga. So choose one. You can take a couple of days to think about it." He crunched into the shell and smiled. "Or I'll choose for you."

That night I couldn't fall asleep. I snuck out of bed and searched *aikido* on YouTube. I saw that it actually had some pretty awesome moves. Who cared about cooperation? This could make me invincible.

And one day, I'd be a black belt!

I grabbed my bathrobe off the floor. I pulled the belt out of its loops and tied it around my waist.

I stood on the bed so I could see myself in the dresser mirror. Not bad!

I still had the belt on when I woke up the next morning.

When Dad came down for breakfast, I said, "Sign me up for aikido."

It had seemed like an easy choice. Now, standing outside the dojo, I realized something. If I wanted to earn a black belt, I was probably going to have to smash other kids to get it. But that meant the other kids who wanted their black belts were going to be smashing *me*.

The book Dad took out of the library should have been more specific about what "building cooperation skills" really meant.

I wondered if it was too late to switch to yoga.

TWO

Seriously, what *was* that smell?

I stretched my foot through the doorway and tested the mat. It squished when I pushed down with my big toe.

Here goes everything.

I stepped into the dojo and looked around. Black-and-white photographs of old Japanese men were hung up on the wall. Blue and red crash pads, bigger and puffier than bed mattresses, slouched in one corner. The walls themselves were white with a few scuffs and dents.

I stood up straight. I finally saw who had been making all the noise. Just two whole kids in the back corner.

On the one hand, I was relieved. If no other kids showed up, I'd only have to survive two boys. On the other hand, I had no idea how to talk to kids like that, kids with so much energy. One of them was taller than me. I put him in seventh or eighth grade. The shorter one was about my height but had big, square shoulders. Maybe a bit older than me—sixth grade? They looked so much alike they had to be brothers. They wore matching jogging pants and T-shirts. And they had matching haircuts too. Buzzed all the way down on the sides, long and floppy on top. Only the cool kids in my school had haircuts like that.

They were still yelling at each other and fighting with everything they had. That included exercise stuff from a set of plastic shelves they had knocked over. Colored balls, hoops and stretchy bands were scattered all around them. A hoop rolled my way, and I casually grabbed it, pretending I wasn't watching them. The shorter boy picked up an orange pylon and tried to smash it against the taller one's head. The taller boy jumped away and picked up a long, yellow elastic band. He whipped it at his brother's bare feet, making him dance around.

"You're going to need more than a plastic hoop if you plan to take on those two," said someone behind me.

I jumped. I turned to see a girl leaning against the back wall. I hadn't noticed her when I came in. She was wearing the same kind of martial arts uniform as me. Except hers obviously hadn't come out of its plastic package right before class.

Her uniform looked broken in. She had her arms crossed, and I could see that her cuffs were pretty worn. Mine were thick and hard. And my sleeves were so long they came all the way down to my fingertips. Her jacket and pants were white, but not blinding. Mine were so bright that my eyes stung if I looked down at them for too long.

I was relieved to see that she was a white belt, like me. But even her belt looked soft and worked in. My belt was so stiff that Dad and I had barely been able to get it tied. We had followed a video on YouTube, folding it and bending it and twisting it over and over again until we'd finally got the right knot. Even so, it had managed to spring itself free only seconds later.

The knot on this girl's belt sat snugly. Mine was already wiggling itself loose, and all I had done was walk into the room. I yanked at the ends of my belt nervously.

The one extra piece she had on was some kind of hoodie helmet. Like the rest of her uniform, it was white. It was made of some expensive-looking fabric with tiny dots all over it. The sides had a pattern of thick little hexagon pads. It hugged her head perfectly, like a futuristic ninja hood.

Her headgear looked awesome, but I wasn't about to say so. She was playing it cool, so I did too. I put on my best bored voice.

"Isn't the helmet a little extreme?" I said. "Or is that some kind of ninja-girl fashion statement?" I tugged my jacket closed to hide my skinny chest. That made the collar scratch against my neck. I shrugged it back, but that made my chest peek out again. Even though I was getting nervous sweaty, I kept up the cool voice. "You're probably a little more worried than me because you're a girl, but I don't think we do punches to the head in aikido. I did some research online."

A massive *thump* came from the corner, and I instinctively ducked. My shoulders stayed tight as I snuck another look at the guys.

"On the other hand…" I said. Maybe it wasn't such a bad idea to have a little extra protection. The videos I'd watched *did* show a lot of throwing. And one person's throwing was another person's falling. I wondered if the headgear came in black. That might distract people from how brand-new my uniform was. It could be a kind of stand-in for a black belt until I got the real thing.

The boys in the corner were now breathing heavily, bent over with their hands on their knees. They'd swipe their long hair out of their eyes to glare at each other, but it would flop back down a second later. They'd try to blow it out of their eyes, but the sweat seemed to make it too heavy and sticky. Maybe they could use some headgear, too, to keep the sweat and the hair out of their eyes.

My shoulders relaxed a little. There was something I could talk to these guys about after all!

The taller kid snagged his little brother in a headlock and ground his knuckles into his skull. "Aikido noogie!" he yelled. "*Aiki-noogie!*"

The shorter one struggled to get free, then reached out and pinched his attacker on the inside of the thigh. His brother yelped and jumped away. They stared at each other again, chests rising and falling.

"They'd better be careful!" the girl said in a bubbly voice. "Without ninja helmets like mine, those losers might knock each other out before class even starts!"

I nodded. "Exactly! I was just thinking the same th—" I looked over at her and stopped cold. Her expression made it clear that she was making fun of me.

The girl turned away to study a row of judo diagrams that were posted on the back wall. Her body flexed as she followed along with the sequences. "By the way," she said, "your pants are on backward."

I looked down. *What!* How? How could you even tell?

As if reading my mind, she added, "It's the kneepads. They go in front. Y'know, because that's where your knees are."

I pulled my right pant leg around to check. Sure enough, I could see a big stitched square of padding.

Right where my knee should be.

Right where my knee would be if my pants weren't on backward.

With all the twisting, my belt knot had come undone again.

But my stomach tied itself in a fresh knot.

The girl put her bubbly voice back on. "Or maybe you're just making some kind of Ninja Boy fashion statement!" She strode away to study another judo poster farther down the row.

Burn.

My first class hadn't even started, and I had already been taken down.

How stupid was I going to look by the time this was over?

THREE

"Let's get ready to ruuumm-ble!"

Another kid bounced into the dojo room. He had a shaved head and a wide smile. He was shorter than any of us, but he looked like he might weigh as much as the two other boys put together.

His uniform was a shining, bright white like mine. Like mine, his sleeves covered his hands down to the fingertips. Because of his round body, though, the front edges of his jacket didn't even come close to covering his wide brown chest. He didn't seem to mind.

He checked me out and then the girl. His eyes moved on to the boys in the corner. I didn't think it was possible, but his smile got bigger.

"*Sumo attack!*" he yelled.

And charged.

I froze.

He blew by me so fast and so close, I felt a breeze.

The brothers looked up. For a second they seemed mesmerized.

At the last second the taller brother dove clear. The shorter one held up his hands uselessly, then almost disappeared from view.

The new kid crushed him like a freight train, burying him in one of the puffy crash pads against the wall.

He raised both hands in victory.

And slowly rolled back and forth, steamrolling the boy with his belly.

I realized my jaw was hanging open. I shut it with a tiny click.

The brother who had escaped was curled up on the floor. He howled in laughter.

The new boy pushed himself away from the crash pad. He smiled again. "I'm Joe!" he said.

The squashed brother slowly peeled himself off the crash pad. Joe grabbed his hand and pumped it.

"I'm Dion," the boy said. He pulled his hand free and backed up a step. He pointed. "That's my big brother, Zack."

Joe put his hands to the sides of his mouth and yelled at the ceiling.

"*Sumo attack! Sumo attack on Zack!*"

He took off, aiming right for Dion's brother.

Launched himself in the air.

Smashed like a wrecking ball.

Zack's laughter came to a muffled stop.

Joe pushed himself up onto his hands and knees. He sat back, kneeling, pausing to catch his breath.

He caught sight of me.

Still breathing heavily, he smiled.

My heart stopped.

It had been kind of shocking but also kind of funny to see the other boys get smothered. The sort of thing that would get a million views online. But it was only okay because they were tough. After all, they had been happily trying to kill each other only a minute before. I bet they could have stopped Joe if they had really wanted to.

But me?

I started to feel the Surge. Tingling fingers, a tight neck and pressure like my head was going to explode. It wasn't about being afraid of getting hurt. I had been roughed up by bigger kids at school before, and I knew that bruises heal.

The real problem, right here, right now, was that I knew exactly how stupid I was about to look. How weak I'd seem when I couldn't laugh off whatever this Joe kid was about to do to me.

He kept me in his sights as he stood up. He got one foot under him, then the other.

He locked his legs straight. Then he pawed at the mats on the floor with one foot. He held up his pointer fingers to the sides of his head like bull's horns.

He ducked his head.

He charged.

The taste of metal washed across my tongue.

I didn't want to play like this. But this kid didn't care. Dad didn't care, or he wouldn't have signed me up for this. Mom didn't care, or she wouldn't have left.

This was how I was supposed to gain confidence and learn cooperation?

I went hot and cold and tense and limp, all at the same time.

Joe yelled for the third time as he raced across the dojo floor.

"*Sumo...*"

The girl in the white ninja hood huffed in disgust.

The huff was a girl noise. The girls in my class made that sound when the teacher told them to run faster in gym class or didn't let them choose their best friends for class projects.

This girl sounded just like them.

But she didn't move like them.

Joe was coming right at me.

The girl pushed off the wall and stepped forward.

Right into the path of the bull. I don't think he could have slowed down if he'd wanted to. And he sure didn't look like he wanted to.

Just as he should have been smashing her, she vanished.

On that exact spot, right in front of me, Joe flipped.

Hard.

The mats shook under my feet, and he landed flat on his back.

He bounced up just a little off the mats, then landed flat again.

The girl rose up from a crouch. She stood over him. "Nice to meet you, Joe. I'm Wafaa."

FOUR

A laugh came from the doorway.

Wafaa stood at attention. Joe, still on the floor and breathing heavily, sat up straighter. I didn't look at Zack and Dion behind me, but I couldn't hear them. For the first time since I walked in, they must have stopped fighting.

A young man stood at the edge of the mats. He wasn't much taller than us, but he had dark stubble that made him look like a teenager, or maybe even a little older. He looked at each of us intensely, one at a time. When he looked at me, I dropped my eyes to the floor. When he moved on to the other kids, I checked him out. He must be our teacher. He had the same uniform jacket as me, but his was even more broken in than Wafaa's. The edges of his cuffs and his jacket were frayed. I could see a bunch of loose little threads.

Instead of pants like ours, he wore a swishy black skirt. It went all the way to his ankles and had long, straight folds down the front.

"I know you're all excited because it's the first class," he said. He kicked off his flip-flops and stepped on the mats. As he did, I saw two of the folds split apart. It wasn't a skirt, after all, but some kind of fancy pants. "I'm excited too." He was holding a gym bag in one hand and a long, skinny black bag in the other hand. He used the long one to point to the mess around Zack and Dion. "But this doesn't happen again. *Ever.*"

Without saying a word Zack started to put the plastic shelves back up. At the same time Dion began picking up all the equipment.

The teacher used his long bag to point at Wafaa now. "Your throw showed excellent technique. Perfect technique, in fact. Which makes me even more excited. Because I'm here to teach technique. You just showed me that you respect that."

The teacher continued. "That was a judo throw, am I right?" Wafaa nodded. She looked proud. "Well, you're not here to practice judo," he said. Wafaa's face fell. "Your parents sent you here to study aikido. So like *that*"—the teacher pointed at Zack and Dion's mess—"judo throws will not happen again in this class. Go help the boys tidy up." He looked at Joe. "Did you catch that? I'm not here to babysit. Whatever it was *you* were doing, it also doesn't happen again. Go help them." I just stood there, stunned.

The teacher walked to the front of the room. "Your parents sent you here to learn aikido technique. My teacher—Kondo Sensei—has told me to make sure you do. You're not here to play games. You're not even here to have fun. Some kids take music lessons and learn piano or violin technique. This is no different."

Something didn't feel right. This guy didn't sound at all like the guy in Dad's library book who'd recommended aikido for stressed-out kids. I raised my hand like you do when you want to say something in school. But the teacher didn't see me.

I cleared my throat, but he still didn't notice. That was usually when I was most comfortable. When I was flying under the radar. This time, though, I thought we'd better get things cleared up before the class got really serious.

"Sir?" I said loudly.

He looked up in surprise, a notebook in his hand. Maybe he hadn't even noticed I was there.

"Call me Sensei," he said. "Sensei Rick."

"Okay…" I said. This guy made me so nervous! "Sensei Rick? You said our parents sent us here to learn technique? But I don't think my dad cares much about technique." I know he was hoping it would help me with my anxiety. But I was also pretty sure that at the very least he would want me to have a little fun. "I think he expected—"

Sensei Rick pointed at me. "Let me stop you right there." He moved his pointing finger to the corner. "Why is it that the rest of them are tidying up, but you're standing here arguing?"

Arguing?

I knew arguing. I had seen my parents argue plenty this past year.

I was being *helpful*. Because he was wrong about why Dad had signed me up. Which meant he might be wrong about why other parents had signed up their kids too. "I think if you just—"

"Are you now going to argue with me about arguing with me?" he asked.

I wasn't sure how to answer. I felt like *he* was the one arguing. *I* was still trying to be helpful. But I also felt like if I said that, he would say I was arguing about arguing about arguing. It started to feel like the kind of round and round argument my parents often had.

"Maybe I'll go help tidy up," I said.

"Too late," called Joe. "All done!" He and the other kids came back over. I was the only one who hadn't made trouble, but somehow I felt like the only one in trouble.

"In that case," Sensei Rick said, "we'd better get started!"

We only did warm-ups and some basic movements that night. But those movements lasted a whole hour and stretched every part of me. Muscles I had never felt before. Muscles I didn't even know existed.

And then came the body slams.

Sensei Rick didn't call them that. He called them "breakfalls." He said that falling down safely was the most important part of aikido. Again, I wasn't so sure we had the same idea about aikido. I didn't see how learning how to fall down was going to help me defend myself. It felt more like learning how to get my butt kicked. I already had that down.

Sensei Rick told us to drop our bums to the mats, then roll backward and kick our legs in the air. At the same time, our arms should reach out and slap the mats.

Before I could ever start to picture how to do this, he dropped.

Boom!

The sound of his arms smashing the mats echoed around the room.

Sensei Rick lay on his back for a second, legs sticking up in the air. Then he tucked them back in and curled into a fast sit-up. He rolled back up to standing as easily as he had fallen down.

It actually looked like it could be fun.

"Ready?" he shouted. "One!"

I took a deep breath.

I threw myself backward at the mats as hard as I could.

The air exploded out of my lungs like two balloons popping. I couldn't suck any air back in. I started to panic. A little voice in my mind protested. *But the mats looked so squishy!*

I lay there, dying, as the ceiling fans spun slowly above me.

Finally, I got breath back in me. I decided to stay down for a few more seconds, just to be safe.

Too late I remembered I was supposed to hit the mats with my arms when I hit the floor. I added them in.

They didn't even hit at the same time.

Pip-pap.

I rolled over onto my belly and took a quick look around. I had only heard one good arm *thump*, and it sure wasn't mine. Aside from that one, everyone else had made little pats like mine.

That was one breakfall.

We did many, many more. Falling down was not as easy as it looked.

At the end of class Sensei Rick told us to kneel down in a line facing him. He knelt at the front of the room, under the photos of the old Japanese men.

"Sitting like this is called *seiza*," he said. "It's a chance to think about what you have learned. Close your eyes and breathe deeply. In through your nose, out through your mouth. In for a count of four. Out for a count of four."

I closed my eyes and inhaled. My uniform was soaked with sweat. My face was burning hot. My chest and back and armpits were on fire. As I inhaled I noticed how heavy my jacket had become on my shoulders. I exhaled and felt the weight grow even heavier.

I inhaled. *How am I ever going to get a black belt if I can barely even do the warm-ups?*

I exhaled. *On the other hand, I'm still alive! I survived!*

"*Mokuso yame!*" Sensei Rick barked. "Open your eyes!" He bowed and told us to go find our parents.

FIVE

I usually jump out of bed and slam the snooze button before I even realize I'm awake.

Today sunlight streamed in through the window, warming my face. It warmed the pillow too, which made it softer, cozier. I fluffed it and smiled.

The warmth from the sun suddenly felt wrong.

My stomach flopped, and my shoulders locked tight.

I never feel the sun on my face when I'm waking up. Never. I shot up and looked around my room. It was way too bright. I looked at the clock: 9:33 AM.

I could see the numbers just fine, but my brain couldn't make sense of them. I stared at the clock, trying to figure out how the green numbers and the warm sun could both be so wrong. It made me queasy. I tried to slow down my breathing.

My alarm goes off at 6:45 AM.

It is 9:33 AM.

Late for school?

Late for school!

The Surge rushed up in full force. Bad taste in mouth. Head squeezed from inside. Throat swelling shut.

I jumped out of bed. I was halfway through stuffing my leg into a pair of jeans when I spotted my T-shirt on the floor. I reached for it, tripping over my jeans. I tried to pop my head through the neck hole, but it was somehow way too small.

What did Dad do to the laundry this time? I was still trying to squeeze my head through when I saw Dad standing in my bedroom doorway, staring at me, head tilted.

"Morning, champ," he said. "Glad you were able to sleep in for a change. Uh, I think that's the arm hole. You look like one of those cats on the internet." He laughed and shook his head.

"They're always getting stuck in places that they don't belong."

I blinked at him through the neck ho—*arm* hole—then peeled the shirt off my head. "You *knew* what time it was?"

When Dad was doing his math stuff for work, he could get into his own dopey zone. Sometimes a few days would go by where he would forget to shop for food. We never ran out, but sometimes dinner got a little weird. One time he made a stir-fry with rice, peas, eggs and bacon, all mixed together. At the last second he dumped in a jar of sweet-and-sour sauce that turned all the rice hot pink. It didn't taste too bad, but it looked like a science experiment gone wrong. The other day I caught him leaving the house in work pants and a pajama top. When I pointed it out, he just shrugged. He just didn't care about the stuff that would bother most people.

So I guess I shouldn't be surprised that he forgot to wake me up.

"You know I hate sleeping in!" I said. "School, Dad! School!"

He smiled and nodded. "I know you love school, son," he said. "So do I. But even I take a break on Saturdays." He paused. "Well, some Saturdays."

I sat down on my bed. I shook my shirt out, found the real neck hole and pulled it on. Got my arms through my sleeves. It still felt like everything was out of order. But the alarm bells ringing in my brain were starting to settle down. I tried again to think it through. *Did I have a spelling test yesterday? Because spelling tests are what we do on Fridays.*

The memory came through the fog.

I did! So yesterday must have been Friday. So today must be Saturday.

I yawned and stretched. My back muscles had a stiffness that I wasn't quite used to. I straightened my arm, and one of my elbows cracked the way some kids crack their knuckles.

It felt good.

I had decided to stick with aikido, at least for the time being. The next few classes had been pretty much the same as the first night's. In some ways they had been less scary, because I had some idea of what I was getting into. But in other ways they were scarier *because* I knew what I was getting into. Then we'd started doing partner techniques, which was scary in a whole other way. But no one had killed me yet.

I was getting to know the other kids a bit better. Wafaa was still being pretty unfriendly to me, and I didn't quite get why. Zack, Dion and Joe still goofed around before every class but were careful not to knock anything over. I didn't get involved, but at our last class I had assigned myself the job of lookout. I'd cleared my throat loudly as soon as I heard Sensei Rick's flip-flops flip-flopping on down the hall. Zack had given me a wink as we lined up.

Sensei Rick had started that class by running us through the warm-ups and basic movements. We weren't spending an hour on them anymore, but we still did them at the beginning of every class. The stances were tricky, feet turned out and knees bent in, arms waving big circles up and down. To me, it felt like learning how to walk all over again. I fell over a bunch of times. Every single time, Wafaa huffed and rolled her eyes. The other boys started laughing so hard that they fell over too, which got *me* laughing, which made me tip over even more.

Sensei Rick had given me a stern look. I'd bitten my lip. I knew it wouldn't stop me from falling over, but I hoped it would at least stop me from laughing.

I didn't think Sensei Rick liked me much. One time I asked him if I could get a drink of water from the fountain in the hall. He just looked at me and told me that if I was that thirsty, I should swallow my own spit.

Ohhhh-kay then.

I didn't tell Dad that last part. I knew if I did, he might try to fix things. And when Dad tried to fix things, he had a way of making them worse.

I flopped back onto my bed. I still had one leg in and one leg out of my jeans.

"I guess the aikido is really tiring you out, huh?" Dad asked. "It's really working! You used to have such bad dreams, but now you're sleeping like a baby!" I couldn't tell if he was more proud of me for doing aikido or of himself for having solved a tricky problem. But my warm pillow felt nice on my neck and the back of my head, so I didn't really care. He smiled as I stretched again. "Why don't we have a lazy day? Maybe a little closer to lunch, we'll go to the mall."

"The mall?" I asked. My raised eyebrows said everything.

He shrugged. "I think it's what normal families do." He thought for a second, then went back downstairs.

Right. Normal families.

Me, a normal kid, and us, a normal family. Just a normal family being normal at the mall.

I dozed off again, the sunlight warm on my face.

SIX

Dad and I stood just inside the mall, looking at the directory map. Nothing had changed. Same stores as always.

"Bookstore?" Dad asked.

I had seen that one coming. "Gaming store?" I asked.

He crossed his eyes, stuck out his tongue and gagged.

Sometimes I wondered which one of us was the real kid.

"How about we go to the gaming store first, then the bookstore?" I said. We both knew it wasn't a real compromise. I only ever went to those two stores. If he could help it, Dad only ever went to one.

He sighed. "Fine, fine. Let's go to the gaming store. We'll see if we can find a way to blow a hundred bucks on some game and later discover that it's impossible to play unless we spend another hundred on game-related upgrades and purchases."

I put on my professor voice. "Well, that is, after all, what 'normal' people *do* at the mall, Dad."

Dad laughed and threw an arm around my shoulders. He might give me a hard time, but I knew he wouldn't hesitate to buy me a new game if I found one I really wanted.

In the gaming store I stood in front of a display that compared two new consoles. It had a big chart that described each one feature by feature.

I was trying to compare them both to a third gaming system when I heard a voice.

I recognized it, but I couldn't pin down whose it was. But it was weird. Usually when I'm thinking that hard, especially when it comes to video games, nothing gets in the way of my focus.

I looked around the store, but I didn't see anyone I knew. Dad was standing just outside the entrance, looking at his phone.

I went back to my research. Figuring out which console was best wasn't as simple as comparing prices. I had to consider which one would let me still play my old games as well as the new games coming out that weren't compatible with the system I had right now. Then there was the question of—

"Aiki-noogie!"

The salesperson behind the counter turned his head sharply. Back corner. Two kids. One tall and one shorter, playing a racing game on a huge screen.

Their backs were to me, but their cool matching haircuts were a dead giveaway.

Zack was grinding the knuckles of his left hand into Dion's head. With his right he deftly steered his controller. On the screen a yellow car slammed into a blue one. The blue one kicked up clouds of digital dust and fat clumps of dirt.

Without taking his eyes off the screen Dion stiff-armed his older brother. In the game the yellow car swerved head on into a wall and exploded into a fireball. In real life Zack lost his balance and bumped into a shelf of empty video-game cases. They toppled and scattered all over the floor.

The real-life crash was more impressive than the video-game one.

Do these two ever stop?

The blue car raced past a checkered line. Fireworks lit up the screen.

"Champion!" Dion yelled. He tossed his controller back onto the demo display and waved to an imaginary crowd.

"You little..." growled Zack. A couple more game cases toppled over as he pulled himself back up.

"You two!" yelled the salesman. "You're dead meat!" He came around from behind the counter, but slipped on one of the loose game cases.

Before he even hit the floor, the boys took off, laughing as they ran. Zack flew right past me, but Dion stopped. He looked surprised.

"Riley!" he said. "I almost didn't recognize you without your white pajamas on!"

I looked nervously at the sales guy. It seemed he had decided to pick up all the cases instead of chasing the boys.

Zack was already long gone. Dion looked back at the salesman too. "Better get out of here, Ry!"

I hesitated. "Maybe we should help..." Dion grabbed my arm and dragged me out of the store.

Dad looked up from his phone. His eyes were glazed. I knew that expression. He was somewhere else, considering the ideas bouncing around in his head. His eyes passed over us as Dion pulled me along with him. Dad looked back down.

Right away, though, he looked back up. I saw him blink as his brain checked back into reality. Just as we were passing, he reached out. He grabbed a handful of my T-shirt, yanking back as Dion pulled me forward.

I was impressed at how strong his grip felt. *Maybe he should try aikido!*

I nearly flew off my feet. Dion *did* fly off his feet, his upper body jerking backward while his legs still ran forward.

Zack poked his head out from behind a pillar. "Riley!" he called and came out from behind the pillar. His expression turned serious when he saw Dad, still holding a fistful of my shirt, and Dion, hanging off my shirt and trying to get his feet back under him. Zack ran at us.

"Wait!" I shouted, sticking both hands out. "Dad! These are my friends! Guys! This is my dad."

"Nice to meet you, sir," Zack said. He stuck out his hand for a handshake.

Dad didn't take it.

He looked from Dion to me to Zack, then back at me. "But you don't have any friends!" he said. Then he let go of my shirt and clapped both his hands over his mouth, eyes wide open. Even he knew how much that made me sound like a total loser.

"Hey!" shouted the salesman from the gaming-store doorway. "Grab those kids!"

We looked at Dad.

"Steal anything?" he asked quickly.

We shook our heads.

"Break anything?"

Again we shook our heads.

"Then," he said, turning, "perhaps we should go." The four of us took off, speed-walking past shoppers and dodging little kids and strollers. We didn't slow down until we hit the food court.

"Oh my gosh!" Dad said, out of breath. He checked over his shoulder. "As the responsible adult here, maybe I should have talked to the salesman." He looked at Zack and Dion sternly. "You really didn't steal or break anything, did you?"

"No, sir!" they said together.

"They just kind of made a mess," I said. "I saw it all happen. It was, like, *kind* of an accident."

Dad looked like he was trying not to smile. He shrugged. "Well, I guess my work here is done." He pulled out his wallet, opened it, wiggled his fingers, then pulled out a twenty-dollar bill. "Why don't you treat your...*friends* to some fries, Riley?" he said. "If you need me, you know where I'll be. If I don't see you before, I'll meet you back here in an hour. Sound good?"

I didn't take the money right away. Dad is generous, but he has never just given me cash and sent me off on my own in the mall before.

Zack nudged me with his elbow. I looked at him.

I guessed I wasn't really on my own this time. I took the cash.

Dad spoke again to the other boys. "As the responsible adult, I should probably ask who you are. I mean, you look familiar. You're from the aikido class, right?" They nodded. "Names?"

"I'm Zack, sir."

"Dion, sir."

This time Dad did shake their hands. "No more trouble for today, right, boys? Accidental or otherwise." They nodded. He looked at me. "One hour." As he turned to head for the bookstore, I saw a funny little smile on his face.

Zack put his arm around my shoulders. "Ry, your dad is very cool. I mean, we get chased out of a store, and he not only runs away with us, but he gives us money for food?" He leaned in closer, his arm around my neck now. "Any chance he wants to upgrade to an older, cooler, better-looking son?"

It was a weak insult. I knew he was joking. The words didn't bother me at all.

I mean, I really did have other friends. We were into the same YouTube channels and video games. Some of them I only knew online. But none of them were jocks who wrestled or threw a football in the hall. We never put our arms around each other like this.

I was getting more and more used to physical stuff at aikido. But there, Sensei Rick always told us exactly what to do—when to strike, how to grab—and even how our partners should react. He always explained carefully whether the attacker should fall backward or sideways or forward. I was starting to notice that the step-by-step explanation was one of the things I really liked about aikido.

But what was I supposed to do with this?

When Zack grabbed me and leaned in, it felt *too* close. The Surge started to creep in. I knew I was being weird, but I felt my shoulders getting tight, and I had to fight not to shove Zack off me. It took me a second to even figure out what he had said.

What would Dion do?

Probably punch him in the privates and gouge his eyes out. I wasn't sure I could pull that off.

Was there an aikido move for this?

I remembered Sensei Rick showing us how to get out of a headlock. He'd taught us to catch the bully's finger and twist it, then duck backward.

That would set you up to grab your attacker's elbow, twist it and push them away.

That seemed like an okay "guy thing" to do.

An aikido thing.

Instead, I decided to risk something else altogether.

"I don't know, Zack," I said. My voice sounded a little too loud in my ears. "If I ever meet this kid, I'll ask him. Until then I guess I'm stuck hanging around with you older, *stupider*, *uglier* nerds."

Dion burst into laughter and pointed at his older brother. "Burn! You're an ugly old nerd!"

Zack laughed too, surprised. Then he got me in a headlock. He gave my neck a quick squeeze, then let go and shoved me away. "Riley's got some sass!" he said.

Dion was still pointing and laughing, so Zack shoved him too and pointed back at him. "That's a burn on you, too, if you think about it! He said ugly *nerds*!"

My risk had paid off.

SEVEN

We got our food and picked out a table. A big box of fries sat between us. Dad had given me enough cash that we could have ordered a small box each, but Zack pointed out that if we shared a box we could get drinks too.

I couldn't believe how cool it was to hang out with these guys. But I was terrified too. I felt like any second I might say or do the wrong thing. Then they'd realize their mistake in deciding to hang with me. Still, I was curious about something. I knew it wasn't a cool thing to ask, but I couldn't stop myself.

"Aren't you scared you'll get in trouble?"

Zack and Dion looked at each other, then at me.

"For what?" Zack asked. I couldn't believe it. Maybe these guys were so tough they really didn't care what they did. Or—the thought, a mean one, came up before I could stop it—maybe they weren't really that bright.

I picked up a french fry and pointed behind me. "I know you didn't mean to, but that was a pretty big mess you made back there."

"Oh, that!" Dion said. He slurped his drink, then nodded. "Yeah, we're *definitely* getting in trouble for that."

He still didn't sound bothered.

It bothered me that they weren't bothered.

I would never be that cool.

Zack saw the look on my face and laughed. "Riley, relax! The guy who works there? That was Yianni! He's our cousin," he said. "He is *definitely* going to tell his mom, and she is *definitely* going to tell our mom, and we are *definitely* going to be in trouble." He shrugged. "But nothing we can do now. So why worry?"

"But Yianni is supposed to keep an eye on us," Dion said. He dragged a whole handful of fries through the ketchup. "And he didn't. So he's going to be in trouble too!" He laughed. "Yianni really *is* an ugly old nerd. He would have kicked us out of the store eventually. He always does."

Zack nodded. He finished his pop and burped. "But since you asked that question," he said, "let me turn it back on you." Zack rattled the ice in his cup, poked at it with his straw and then pulled the straw out and pointed it at me. "Aren't *you* afraid that *you're* going to get in trouble?"

I could feel my ears burning. I was already feeling guilty, and I didn't even know what he was talking about.

"For what?" I said. "I didn't knock anything over!" I looked at Dion. "Or knock *anyone* over! Are you going to say I did?" I had vouched for them with my dad. I couldn't believe that now they were going to tell on me.

"No, dummy," Zack said, frowning. "At aikido."

"Oh," I said. Now I was really confused.

I mean, I did seem to kind of get in trouble at aikido a lot. It felt like Sensei Rick was always picking on me for something. Is that what they meant?

"Well, sometimes Sensei talks for too long when he's showing us something," I said. "It gets boring when he makes us do the same thing over and over and over."

A couple of times, when I'd spaced out or when I really was trying hard but wasn't getting the technique just right, Sensei Rick had said I was just being lazy. One time he even sent me to the corner for a time-out, just like a kindergarten baby. "I guess I'm getting used to it," I said, trying to copy Zack. "Sensei doesn't like me. But it's out of my hands. So why worry?"

Zack waved this off. "All of us get in trouble for goofing off sometimes," he said. "I'm not talking about that. I'm talking about Wafaa."

My ears lit right back up, faster than a Christmas tree. I still didn't know exactly what Zack was talking about, but I knew Wafaa didn't seem to like me much either. The friendlier I tried to be, the madder she seemed to get. She was careful never to hurt me when we were partnered up, even though she was good enough to destroy me if she wanted to. But I did worry that if she got any madder, one day she just might.

"Well, what did I ever do to her?" I asked. Obviously, they knew something I didn't.

"You're always making jokes about her 'ninja hood,'" Dion said around a mouthful of fries. "You never shut up about it."

"Those aren't jokes!" I said. "I mean, they're not *mean* jokes. I like the headgear. I'd wear it. The mats are soft, but our falls are already getting harder. I was going to say you guys should get some too. It would help you with the..." I quickly wiped the ketchup off my fingers, then gave my head a big flip and pretended to swipe long hair off my forehead.

They laughed and flipped their hair. I reached for another fry and decided to put something out there. "I don't know if there's a sports store that sells them in the mall, but maybe when my dad comes back, we could see about getting matching ones." I quickly stuffed the fry into my mouth.

Once I'd said it out loud, I could tell by their faces it was a stupid idea. I stared at the table, chewing like crazy while I waited for their answer.

They didn't say anything for a few seconds. I looked up, and they were staring at me.

"You're really not joking, are you?" Zack said.

"I was thinking we could get black ones!" I said. Just in case they thought Wafaa's white one looked girlie. "Or not. Whatever. It's stupid. Forget I said it."

They looked at each other for a moment, and then Zack spoke up. He didn't sound mean, but it was like he was talking to a little kid. "Riley, it's not a helmet."

"And it's definitely not a *ninja hood*," said Dion. Zack elbowed him.

"I know it's not *actually* a ninja hood!" I said. "But it's padded. It is like a helmet." There was something I wasn't getting.

"Yeah, Riley...but no. It's not. Wafaa is Muslim. It's her head cover. Her whaddayacallit."

"It's a *hijab*, stupid!" Dion said to his brother. He elbowed him back. "Don't you know anything?"

Dion wasn't saying that to me. But as soon as he put it that way, the Surge squeezed my stomach. I nearly threw up all the fries right there on the table.

My brain started flashing to every time I had stupidly called it a ninja hood.

Every time I had called her Ninja Girl.

My brain replayed every time I had said her "helmet" looked great and that I wanted one too.

I had meant it that time I asked her how much it cost and where she got it and if it came in different colors.

Now the look on her face made sense. It was a mad face. And just for a flash of a second, she had looked really...hurt.

Of course I knew what a hijab was!

I just didn't recognize hers. The girls in my school who had them had these long scarves that wrapped around and around. Some of the girls wore ones that were pink or yellow or had colorful prints on them.

Wafaa's is padded! I wanted to shout at Zack and Dion. *It's stretchy! It's made from the same stuff as sports shirts!*

The fries felt like a greasy ball in my gut.

I leaned my head on my hand.

I hated myself for even thinking it, but the thought came on strong.

Maybe I was the one who wasn't so bright.

EIGHT

A few more classes went by. I knew I had been a jerk to Wafaa, but I didn't apologize to her. I didn't know what to say, so I just didn't say anything.

We were getting to the end of June, and that meant summer vacation. Part of me hoped that Sensei Rick would shut down classes for the summer. I thought that maybe by the end of the summer Wafaa would have forgotten all about it. But when I asked Dad, he said that Sensei Rick had told parents classes would be offered as usual through July and August.

I couldn't stop replaying all the things I had said to Wafaa about her hijab. They sounded worse and worse every time.

At home I stalled with any excuse I could think of, so I didn't have to hang around with her on the mats before class. *Dad! I can't find my belt! Where did you put it this time?* Being late to anything was one of my Surge triggers, but the idea of filling empty time with Wafaa was worse than the risk of being late.

I guessed she didn't want to see much of me either, because she was always the first to leave the mats at the end of class, right on the heels of Sensei Rick's flip-flops.

I threw all my nervous energy into doing aikido. Everyone had the uniform now, and we had gotten really good at doing the warm-ups all together. At each class we started by jumping up and down, back and forth, and side to side. Then we reached and stretched to one wall, then to the other. I wasn't even tipping over anymore. Not even when we bent forward as far as we could, then bent backward until we could see the back wall, upside down, behind us.

Every movement fit into a count of eight. It didn't matter if we were stretching our wrists—

four different ways!—or spinning our bodies around like they were in a tornado. It was always to a count of eight. Sensei Rick yelled out in Japanese, *"Ichi! Ni! San! Shi! Go! Roku! Shichi! Hachi!"*

I put my hands on my hips and wiggled them in big circles, first in one direction, then the other. It was hard to do that one without giggling.

Especially when Joe said, "Here comes the crowd pleaser!" under his breath.

But he stopped saying it after Sensei Rick overheard him once. Sensei Rick stopped the class and made Joe do push-ups. Ten of them. One for each year of his age. I couldn't stop giggling at Joe, so then I had to do the push-ups too.

"Riley!"

Oops. I had spaced out again.

I came back to attention, nodding as if I had been carefully thinking about Sensei Rick's words.

"Well?" he asked.

I bit my lower lip and looked at the photographs of the old Japanese senseis. I tried to look as if I was super close to answering his question. That would be impressive, considering I had no idea what the question actually was.

Sensei Rick exhaled loudly and looked at the ceiling. "Okay, just go with Wafaa and Joe and you three can take turns practicing the technique."

Go with Wafaa? My stomach squeezed into a tight ball. I put my hand up.

"Too late!" he said. "You had a choice, but I had to make it for you! Wafaa and Joe!"

Zack put his hand up. "I could go with Wafaa," he said. He blushed a little. "Or Joe or whatever."

I wondered why Zack didn't ask for me.

Even though he hadn't picked me, I still thought I'd rather go with him and Dion. I put my hand up.

But Sensei Rick was shaking his head at Zack. "You and Dion can work together. You guys are so rough, no one else wants to work with you."

Not true!

I started waving my hand and bouncing on my knees a little. I'd go with them in a heartbeat.

Wafaa elbowed me before Sensei Rick could see me. "You're a slow learner!" she whispered. "Just do what Sensei says!"

I put my hand down and stared at the mats.

Joe pounded me on the back. "Don't worry, Ry! We won't go too hard on ya!"

The three of us stood up. Wafaa took charge.

"First I'll attack Joe, and he can throw me. First from his right side, then from his left. Then, Riley, you attack me, and I'll throw you, right and left. Then, Joe, you attack Riley, and he can throw you, both sides. Okay?" She didn't wait for an answer. "Good."

The thing I liked about doing it in this order was it would let me watch Joe and Wafaa do the technique for the first time. I could see how the throw was supposed to go.

Plus they'd be showing me how to fall out of it. Sensei Rick had said that falling safely was the most important part of aikido. That's why we practiced our breakfalls so much. The more techniques we learned, the more I was understanding what he meant. Different throws and pins could send the attacker flying in different directions. It made a big difference if you knew whether to fall forward, backward, sideways or straight down!

Wafaa and Joe bowed, then faced each other in *kamae*, the basic stance. Wafaa attacked, punching right at Joe's chest.

Instead of standing still and blocking, Joe moved straight in to meet Wafaa. With an open hand, he reached past her fist and scooped her arm out sideways. Even though he was a pretty heavy kid, he had the smoothest moves of all the boys.

Wafaa had really put her weight into the punch. But when it didn't land on any target, the power of the punch carried her off-balance. She tilted sideways where Joe had guided her and hopped on one foot as she tried not to fall. Just as she found her balance, Joe stepped straight at her. He kept his arm stiff and swung it up. The heel of his hand connected with her chin. He shuffled forward one last time, driving her chin up, back and then down.

If he had been holding a cream pie, it would have been pure comedy.

But this was no pie-in-the-face routine. It was a serious martial arts move. Wafaa's head tipped backward and her body followed. She rose up on her toes, stalled, then totally lost it, smashing down into the mats with a loud breakfall.

She bounced up, smiling.

Great timing. Great teamwork.

I laughed loudly. Joe's stiff-armed shove had reminded me of when Dion shoved Zack into the video-game shelves at the mall. It had worked pretty well there too.

We were learning some useful self-defense after all!

Wafaa looked at me. She lost her smile. "Is it *that* funny to see me knocked down?" she asked. "Keep laughing. In a minute it's going to be my turn to throw *you*."

My chest tightened and my throat closed. I wasn't laughing anymore.

Joe and Wafaa worked through the technique a second time. Wafaa punched with her other hand, and Joe led her out to his other side. The technique ended exactly the same way. A hand to the chin, a body to the mats.

She bounced up again. She wasted no time going into *kamae* stance.

Joe sat down a safe distance away, and I got up to face Wafaa. I did *kamae* too.

My turn to attack.

Wafaa's turn to defend.

I closed my right hand into a fist. I looked into her eyes. She stared back at me, but her eyes didn't reveal any feelings.

I stepped and punched. It was a lot slower and a lot lighter than it needed to be. This was partly to show I really wasn't out to get her. That I wanted to play nice.

But I was also scared. We had learned early on that in aikido the person doing the technique uses the attacker's power against him. The harder I punched, the harder I'd fall.

Today I punched pretty softly.

Wafaa frowned and slapped my fist away without doing the rest of the moves. Her message was clear. My wimpy punch didn't deserve an aikido technique.

"*Punch* me," Wafaa said quietly, so Sensei Rick couldn't hear. "Don't worry. I know what to do with it!"

I took a deep breath. If this was what it took to prove that I respected her, I was going to give it everything I had.

Again I made my hand into a fist.

Found my target on her lower chest.

And gave it everything I had.

BAM!

I heard the sound of me hitting the mats before I felt it.

Next thing I knew, I was looking up at the ceiling.

It wasn't that she had knocked me out. It was that her timing had been perfect.

I had gone from vertical to horizontal faster than my brain could follow. She had used everything I had put into the punch against me. And I hadn't held anything back.

I tried to feel out my body. My palms stung from slapping the mat, and my chest felt like someone had pounded it like a drum. But I hadn't hit my head, and nothing actually hurt. Lying there, I just felt weird somehow.

I usually didn't like the endless breakfalls we did in every class, but right then I was grateful for them. All that practice had kept me safe.

And that's when I noticed it.

That was the weird feeling.

I felt safe.

I rolled over and jumped back up. Zack and Dion had stopped to see if I was okay. Sensei Rick had been helping them, but he'd also stopped what he was doing. He looked like he had been about to run over to check on me. I could see that Joe had crawled a little closer, and Wafaa, for the first time since I'd met her, looked nervous.

Standing, I threw my arms in the air.

"And the crowd goes wild!" I yelled.

I wanted to let everybody know I was okay. I wanted to let them know that I was more than okay. I hadn't just survived the hardest throw I had ever taken. I had gotten back up and I was ready to go again. I was more than ready. I was ready *plus*. I had gotten back up *plus*.

I smiled at Wafaa. "I still owe you a punch from my other side," I said. "You think you can handle it?"

She nodded slowly, thinking it over. Finally she smiled. "Let's see what you're made of, Little Ninja," she said.

On the other side of the mats, I noticed Sensei Rick smile too.

NINE

As usual, when it was time for class to end, Sensei Rick called for us to line up. That night we were a very sweaty row of kneeling students.

As usual, we bowed to the front of the room. This showed we were thankful for the chance to train.

As usual, we bowed to Sensei Rick. This showed we were grateful to him for teaching us.

As usual, he bowed back to show he was grateful to us for coming here to train. Finally, he shouted, "*Osu!*" This was an akido word that showed respect. We shouted it back.

But there was nothing usual about what Sensei Rick said next.

"Great workout tonight, guys," he said. "I mean it." That in itself was weird. He did not hand out compliments often. "There are a couple of things coming up that you need to know about."

Uh-oh. My neck started to feel tight. I hated surprises.

"First, soon we will be going on a little trip."

This made as much sense to me as if Sensei Rick had started speaking to us in Japanese. *Who's going on a trip? Where?*

"You've heard me mention my teacher, Kondo Sensei. What you may not know is that he has a ninth-degree black belt in Yoshinkan aikido. Only one other person in the whole world has attained that level." He pointed at one of the black-and-white photos on the wall above him. "Only one other person has gone past it."

Wow. Ninth degree. I wondered how long it would take me to get there.

"For most of the summer Kondo Sensei lives at his cottage, which is just over an hour's drive from here. He even has a little dojo up there. Twice a year he runs an aikido training camp for adult students."

My feet were falling asleep from kneeling for so long. Pins and needles were tickling like crazy. I started to wiggle around to get them out. I wished he would just get to the point!

"And here's the part I can't quite believe. He has invited all of *you* to come up to his cottage for a mini training camp. Just you kids. For a weekend."

I stopped wiggling.

We stared at him.

Wafaa finally broke the silence.

"Sensei Rick, my parents would never—"

Sensei Rick smiled and raised his hand. "I've already been in touch with all of your parents. I emailed them all the info they need and then some. This is a real camp. Kondo Sensei taught children's classes for many years, long before you guys came along."

Dad knows about this?

There had to be some misunderstanding. With everything that had happened with Mom leaving, there was no way Dad would let me go overnight anywhere. I looked up and down the line, and the rest of the kids looked just as skeptical.

"I have to say, this isn't exactly the reaction I expected." Sensei Rick looked a little disappointed. "Your parents have all told me you can go if you want to. They would have told you themselves, but I wanted to see the look on your faces when you heard the news." He shrugged. "You don't have to come if you don't want to. It's not for a couple of weeks, and nobody's paid any fees or handed in the trip forms yet. But trust me—this is a trip you don't want to miss. It's beautiful up there, there's lots of things to do, and you will have a chance to train with one of the world's best. Doesn't that sound even a little bit fun?"

He almost seemed sad. I didn't know how I felt about the idea of being away from Dad for an entire weekend, but it did sound like it could be a little fun.

"Woo-hoo!" Joe shouted. He punched the air. Zack and Dion high-fived. Wafaa had a small smile on her face.

"That's more like it!" Sensei Rick said. "I know you'll find this hard to believe, but even I relax a little when I'm up at the camp!" He laughed. "I've got one other special announcement." He hesitated.

"But maybe I'll save that news for when we're up there." He smiled, bowed again and said, "*Osu!*"

Our five voices called out "*Osu!*" as we bowed back to him. He made his way off the mats, pausing briefly to get his flip-flops on.

As soon as he was out of the room, the boys started yelling.

"This is going to be awesome!" Joe said.

"A whole weekend without Mom and Dad!" Zack crowed.

"I wonder how hard the mats are at this dojo," I said.

Wafaa didn't say anything. She picked up her bag and made for the door.

"Hey!" I called. "Aren't you excited about this trip, Wafaa?"

She turned, smiled and shrugged. "Sure," she said. "I just find it hard to believe that my parents will let me go up to some cabin in the woods with four stinky boys for the weekend. But if they really say I can go—which I doubt—I'll think about it." She bowed at the edge of the mats and stepped backward out the door.

She was still not being very friendly. I'd thought we had finally broken the ice between us with the last exercise. It had seemed like she was enjoying herself. Now she was back to ignoring us.

Joe had untied his belt and was trying to cool himself off by waving his jacket open and shut. I watched another drop of sweat roll off his shaved head. The fanning wasn't helping. "What's the problem, Ry?" he asked, dragging his sleeve across his forehead. "Great class, great news!"

"Exactly!" I said. "We just had a great class. We just heard great news. So why can't Wafaa be happy? The class wasn't just great. It was awesome. You threw her, she threw me, I threw you. We all got our butts kicked, and we all kicked some butt, right?"

"C'mon, Riley," Zack said, rolling his eyes. "Not everything's about you. Do you really think you're the reason she has a hard time being in aikido?"

I threw my hands up. "How do I know? At first I didn't think her bad mood had anything to do with me! I thought I was being friendly! Then you told me that it was all my fault."

Dion shook his head.

"No, Ry," Zack said. "We told you to stop bugging her about her...uh..."

"Hijab!" Dion said.

"I *know*," Zack said. "I just forget the word sometimes. Jeez." He frowned. "But no, Riley, you are not the reason she's unhappy here." He worked his belt knot loose as he spoke. He looked at me again when it came free in his hands. "I mean, you definitely didn't help, but once you figured it out, that was fine."

"I know, I know," I said. "So what else?"

"What else what?" Joe asked. He had given up on fanning himself and now lay flat on the floor.

"What else is making her so unhappy? Class is not so bad!"

I thought about how focused Wafaa was even when we were doing our basic movements. She always put her feet at the right angles and never got her hands mixed up. She was the only one who never spun around too much or fell over before a throw came. She never cross-stepped into left-side *kamae* when we were just supposed to shuffle forward in right-side. To get out of an armlock, the rest of had just learned forward rolls. But Wafaa could already do forward flips to escape. Sensei Rick hadn't even shown us that yet.

"She's so good, but she never looks happy to be here," I said. "Are we so awful to be around?"

"It's not about you," Zack said again. "It's not about *us*."

"Look," Dion said. "We know Wafaa from school. I mean, we see her around, but we don't *know* her know her. She's in between our grades. But one day I was showing my friends one of our wrist locks. *This* one."

He grabbed Joe's hand. Joe, still flat on the floor, was too tired to care. Dion twisted his wrist and bent it backward, then let go. It flopped down loudly on the mats.

"So I'm telling them all about aikido. Turns out there's a kid in my class who does judo here. When I say Wafaa's one of the kids in aikido, he says she used to be in his judo class. And that she was amazing. She kicked everybody's butt, girls and boys. And they aren't just all white belts in there. They even have kids who are *brown* belts. He says that Wafaa got up to green belt, but something went wrong, and she just quit."

"Hmmm," I said. That explained why she was so good at the flips and falls.

I looked up at the judo pictures on the back wall. They reminded me of our first night here, how Wafaa had paid so much attention to them. And how she had taken out Joe.

But that got me wondering. "So if she was so good at judo, why did she leave it?" I asked. "Why start all over with a white belt in aikido?"

"This kid said she left judo because of some new girl coming in. And maybe something to do with her hoodie? She didn't always have one, you know. She only started wearing it, like, last year."

Zack didn't miss his chance. "Hey, Mr. Know-It-All. It's not called a hoodie! It's called a hijab!"

The guys had only been trying to help me understand, but the more I learned about Wafaa, the worse I felt.

I said goodbye and left the dojo. In the lobby I passed a judo bulletin board. I had never stopped to look at it before. It was covered in photographs.

Each of the kids wore a uniform that looked just like ours, except some were blue instead of white. The kids had different belt colors. White, yellow, orange, green, blue and brown. Only the adults in the pictures had black belts. One grown-up, maybe the top sensei, had a red belt. There were pictures of the kids standing on podium after podium, getting medal after medal, hugging trophy after trophy. This club won a lot of tournaments.

So many winners, and they all look so happy. What went wrong for you, Wafaa?

Suddenly there she was. Her smile was so big that my eyes had passed right over her at first.

And it wasn't just her smile that made her tough to recognize. She didn't have her hijab on. Her hair was dark and pulled back.

I leaned in closer to make sure. I covered up her hair with my hand. I had never seen Wafaa looking that happy, but this was definitely her.

A green belt was tied around her waist, just like Joe said, and a gold medal was around her neck. The sensei with the red belt stood beside her, arm around her shoulders. His smile was just as wide as hers.

She looked so different here. It wasn't just that she had a colored belt and a medal, or that I could see her hair. It was that look on her face, her looking so happy.

We had been training together for a couple of months, but I had never once seen her look like that.

I wondered if I ever would.

TEN

The next two weeks flew by. We were all on our best behavior. No one wanted to be told they couldn't come on the trip. I kept waiting for Sensei Rick to tell us how good we were being, but he never said anything. He just seemed suspicious at first, like he was on the lookout for trouble. Then he seemed relieved.

I had read books and seen movies about kids who went to camp. I had always thought it looked awful. All those...*cheerful* kids. Always doing... *activities*. Never sitting on a couch and playing video games or just hanging out, doing nothing.

At least this will be with kids I like!

The morning of our trip finally came.

I had packed and repacked a few times. Just as Dad started backing the car out of the driveway, I panicked, thinking I'd forgotten my belt. I tore my duffel bag apart, then made Dad pull back up to the house. I ran inside while Dad stuffed everything into my bag again.

I rushed up to my bedroom. I dumped my laundry basket upside down. A couple of dirty T-shirts and some underwear fell out, but no belt. I kicked the pile around just to be sure. I dropped to the floor and checked under my bed. I could see a comic I had lost a month earlier, stuck between the wall and another T-shirt, but that was it. I grabbed the T-shirt and stood up. I twisted the shirt in my hands. I tried to calm down and remember the last place I had seen the belt.

Then I saw something that made me forget all about it. There, stapled on the corkboard over my desk. My best picture of Mom.

It wasn't from a birthday or Christmas or any other special day. Just a random day. All three of us were out for a drive. We'd passed a sign that said *Cherries 4 Sale*, and Mom braked and pulled over.

An old man in a straw hat was sitting under a cherry tree, selling the fruit for five dollars a basket. Mom gave him some money but said she wanted to pick her own. She didn't even wait for an answer. She just grabbed a bucket from the grass, climbed up the tree and started pulling on the branches. The old man watched her from his chair, cheering her on. Dad and I almost died laughing. Dad pulled out his phone and got Mom to sit still for a second so he could get a shot of her up in the tree, holding the bucket.

"I found the belt!" Dad yelled from the bottom of the stairs. His voice jolted me back to reality. "It's down here! It was stuck inside your uniform pants the whole time!"

I ran downstairs and out to the car. I buckled up as Dad backed out of the driveway again. I checked the clock on the radio. We were definitely late.

"Can we go fast?"

"No problem, bud," Dad said. He shifted from *Reverse* into *Drive* and hit the gas. He knew how much I hated to be late. "What's that?" he asked, glancing down at my lap.

I looked down. The picture of Mom was in my hand. I hadn't even noticed that I had grabbed it. I folded it in half and shoved it deep into my pocket.

"Nothing."

I held my breath when he didn't say anything for a few seconds.

"Picture of Mom?" he asked.

I took a few seconds before answering. "Yeah."

He put his hand on my shoulder, stared ahead at the road and didn't say another word.

We pulled into the parking lot ten minutes late. Sensei Rick and the other families were already there. I silently prayed that I wouldn't have to do push-ups for being late, right there on the asphalt in front of all the parents and the other kids.

But no one seemed to notice we were late, and no one seemed in a hurry to leave. The only kid without parents there was Wafaa. I asked Joe where they were. They had been there, he said, but had just left.

Joe's mom and dad were a lot quieter than I'd expected them to be, considering how loud Joe is. I had thought they'd both be brown, like him, but I was wrong. His dad had much darker skin. He kept rubbing his son's shaved head and talking to him quietly. I couldn't hear what he was saying, exactly, but I could tell he had a bit of an accent. His mom was white. She patted Joe's shoulder every few seconds. She didn't look upset, but I noticed she had bunched-up tissues in her hand. I wondered if she had an accent too.

Zack and Dion's mom flipped back and forth between wiping tears from her eyes and yelling at the boys in Greek. I got closer to Dion and asked what she was saying. He said she was pretty sure the brothers were going to get in some kind of trouble, and she was telling them off for it ahead of time, reminding them of how much trouble they'd be in when they got home.

Dad came up and clapped me on the shoulder. He pulled me in a for a big hug. "Be good! Have fun! Be safe!" he said loudly.

I saw the other kids climbing into the minivan. I hugged him back.

He looked me in the eye. "I love you, Riley," he said. "And I miss Mom too. But you deserve to have a great time with your friends. So go have some fun!" He pulled me in for one more rough hug, then spun me around and pushed me toward the minivan.

Sensei Rick was standing at the back of the van. I handed him my duffel bag, and he tossed it on top of the pile. I turned my head and pretended to cough, but really I was wiping away a tear. It was going to be hard to be away from my dad, I realized.

I climbed in the side door and grabbed the last open seat, in the middle, beside Joe. Zack and Dion had the whole back row, and Wafaa was up front in the passenger seat.

The parents stood in the parking lot, waving as we pulled out. We waved and yelled back, and everyone's spirit was so contagious that I soon forgot my tears.

ELEVEN

Because we were yapping and laughing so much, I didn't notice that we had left the big highway. We passed through a small town. The space between houses grew into wide grassy lawns that I'd never seen in the city. The lawns gave way to even bigger farms. Dirt and crops filled the huge spaces between the orange-brick farmhouses. Water cannons blasted rows and rows of green plants.

We slowed as the road cut through another small town. Instead of paved driveways, most of these houses had gravel out front. A few of them had tractors parked beside family cars and pickup trucks. The yards had rough wooden fences and were decorated with wagon wheels.

The town gave way to country again. We sped up and cruised the long, curving stretches. A group of motorcycles roared past us on the wrong side of the road. Joe made faces through the window at them, and one of the riders caught him. He slowed for a second to match our speed, then pulled down the red bandanna that had been covering his face. He stuck out his tongue at us. Then he gave us the thumbs up, smiled and took off.

We shouted at every cow, sheep and horse that we passed. We pinched our noses and waved our hands and complained at their stink. After an hour or so a row of five or six giant metal windmills rose in the distance. They had long spikes for arms, which turned slowly. They looked like something that might have fallen off an alien ship.

The sunlight and all the time in the minivan were making me dopey. I almost fell asleep, but a sharp bend in the road jolted me awake. Then Sensei Rick slowed right down and turned off the highway. The van bumped along a gravel road.

We drove through a tunnel of trees with long grass on either side. Here, Sensei Rick drove super slow. He rolled down the windows and told us we could stand up and stick our hands out. We high-fived maple leaves and let cedar needles tickle our arms.

The gravel road ended at a small house. The cottage. It wasn't as big as a city house, but it had a huge wooden porch that ran all the way around it.

The grass had been cut short around the cottage. Sensei Rick drove right on the grass alongside the house. We passed a tree with a beat-up tire swing turning in the breeze.

"On their first time here, most people usually start opening the doors before the van even stops!" he said, as he threw the van into *Park*. "What are you waiting for?"

Joe and I each yanked open the side doors, and we all climbed out.

Behind the house was grass and more grass. I couldn't believe how green and soft it was. And how big and empty and blue the sky was. It never looked this...*big* and...well, *empty* in the city. A few puffs of white cloud floated around like they had nothing better to do on a sunny afternoon.

If we were in the city, this would be the cottage's backyard.

But we weren't in the city. And it wasn't a backyard. It was as big as a city park.

Five worn-out trailers were spread out around the field. They sat at odd angles to one another, like wagons making a circle in those old cowboy movies.

I heard a tiny buzzing and looked up to see a small airplane moving across the sky.

I wondered what we looked like to the pilot. To me, looking across to the other end of the field where the grass just disappeared, it felt like we were at the edge of the world.

All the energy that had built up in the car ride exploded in my legs. I sprinted across the field, heading right for the edge. I needed to know what was beyond the edge of the world. My feet flew along, and my lungs burned with fresh air.

As I got closer, a lake appeared. The closer I got, the bigger it got. Soon I could tell it was as wide as the sky above it. I slowed down as I ran out of grass. I was on a small cliff that overlooked the lake. The only thing protecting me from the edge was an old fence. Each section had one piece of driftwood for a top rail and one for a bottom rail. Some of the pieces were crooked but pretty much lined up from one stretch to the next. The whole thing was held together with long twists of wire at each post. Right out of the Old West.

I realized that ever since I had jumped out of the van, I had been hearing the sound of waves. They were far away at first, just a layer of blank noise in the background. I had listened for a second and thought it was the buzzing of bugs and empty country space. Now that I was at the cliff's edge, I could clearly hear the soft sounds of the waves building, rushing and easing off.

Building, rushing, easing off.

Building, rushing, easing off.

I could almost feel them moving through me.

Far out in the lake I could see a lighthouse on a tiny island. Seagulls flew in spirals all around it. A few waves broke up into white fizz at the edges of the island, but row after row after row of waves, farther and longer than I could see, rolled right past it. They didn't care that the lighthouse was there.

Right in front of me, just on the other side of the fence, there was really long grass for a couple of feet, then a drop.

I climbed on the fence's bottom rail and leaned forward to get a better look. There were spots where the cliff face bumped out into sandy little landings. A broken handrail and a few wooden steps showed that someone had carved a path at some point.

I leaned farther forward. At the bottom of the cliff was a rocky beach. A few pointy boulders stuck out of the lake where the water met land.

Then the fence shifted suddenly, and the piece I was standing on dropped a couple of inches. I grabbed the top rail and squeezed. A splinter dug into my hand and my heart jumped.

"Move it, slowpoke!"

"You're going down!"

Zack and Dion were running toward me. I could hear their feet pounding. They had gotten a much slower start out of the van and were making up for it by racing each other to the edge. Each ran with an arm stuck out. Zack's long legs got him there first, and he laughed as he slapped the wood, gasping.

Dion, a few seconds behind him, slammed into the same section of fence.

Right where he slammed, the top rail flew off. It went over the edge, bouncing, falling, bending the tiny plants and skinny trees on the cliff face. Dion almost followed, spinning his arms like the windmills we had seen on the road. He tried to catch a fence rail that wasn't there anymore.

Zack grabbed a fistful of his brother's shirt and hauled him back.

The three of us stared as the wood tumbled down. It caught on a rock, then flipped and rolled again. A fist-sized chunk of wood splintered off. Finally, it rolled to a stop on rocks below.

Zack and Dion weren't twins, but the look on their faces was identical.

"Holy *crap*," I whispered.

They turned and looked at me.

Very gently I stepped down.

TWELVE

Joe joined us, huffing and puffing. Wafaa followed easily behind him. They looked at Zack and Dion with wide eyes before looking over the edge.

"You are in *trou-ble!*" sang Joe.

It looked like their mom had been right to yell at them ahead of time. We had been here less than ten minutes, in an almost totally empty field, and they had *still* found a way to bust up the place. And almost thrown themselves off a cliff in the process.

"AY, *OSU!*" a voice boomed behind us.

The five of us turned around. I didn't know if it was out of habit or a real effort to show respect, but Wafaa bowed deeply, just as if we were in class.

Kondo Sensei.

It had to be.

He was all the way across the field, standing on the back deck of the cottage, but he sounded as powerful as a giant. It was a voice that could turn any place into a dojo.

The way he was dressed, though, was a different story. He had on a red plaid shirt with rolled-up sleeves. It hung untucked over baggy shorts with saggy pockets.

Was this Kondo Sensei?

Before today, I had never seen Sensei Rick out of an aikido uniform, and he'd been teaching us for almost two months.

"NO BACK BREAKFALLS GONNA HELP YOU IF YOU FALL OVER THERE!"

Yep. That's a sensei.

Sensei Rick came up beside him to see what the fuss was about. He was just a couple of inches taller than Zack, but even from here I could see that Kondo Sensei was much shorter than him. The top of his black buzz cut came to just past Sensei Rick's shoulders.

Even though he was probably about my height, Kondo Sensei was wider than Sensei Rick in the shoulders and chest. It was no wonder he had such a powerful dojo voice.

I was sure this was not the first impression Sensei Rick had wanted us to make in front his teacher. He took a step toward us and opened his mouth, to start yelling, I figured, but Kondo Sensei put a hand on his arm. Sensei Rick looked at him, and Kondo shook his head. Sensei Rick closed his mouth.

I hadn't seen *that* in the dojo before. Shutting up Sensei Rick was one aikido technique I'd have to learn before the weekend was over.

Kondo Sensei waved for us to come back to the cottage.

"*HAPPY TO SEE YOU!*" he bellowed as we got closer. He pointed to the minivan. Sensei Rick was now unloading it, tossing our bags into a pile.

"Take your bags, go find beds. Have a nap, relax. In a couple of hours we're gonna train." Kondo Sensei looked out at the open field with a smile.

"It's gonna be *hot*," he continued. "Next couple of days, you're gonna *sweat*! That's summer *gasshuku*!

That's Japanese martial arts tradition! We're gonna work hard, have fun, roast marshmallows! Let's *GO!*" He turned and stepped back into the cottage, sliding the door shut behind him.

We looked at Sensei Rick.

"You heard the man," he said. "Get your bags, then grab some beds."

We looked at one another. *What beds?*

"Uh, Sensei Rick?" called Wafaa. A breeze from the lake blew the corner of her hijab across her face. It was light blue, with small yellow flowers. She tucked it back into place as she looked around.

"Yes?" he answered.

"Where do we…uh, *go?*"

"These are the bags," he said, pointing to the pile at his feet. He waved his hand toward the trailers spread around the camp. "Those are the beds. Pick one." I was surprised that he wasn't going to tell us who was supposed to sleep where, or at least give us a tour of the trailers. It was a lot more freedom than I was used to. Sometimes I wondered if he thought that kids were just smaller adults. "Students in the trailers, teachers in here."

He nodded at the cottage. He smiled a goofy smile. "It's my first time staying in the teacher's cottage."

For a second I was happy for him.

Then he blew it.

"I'll have a fridge, air conditioning, Wi-Fi," he said. "But you guys enjoy it out here in the 'lunch boxes.'" He waved his arm again at the trailers. "Take your pick. You can each have your own, or you can double up. Each trailer has two little bedrooms and a bathroom. You can use the showers, but it's lake water, so don't drink it. Kondo Sensei said he put a case of bottled water in each one." He lifted his own bag from the pile. "I suggest you drink as much water as you can. Kondo Sensei wasn't kidding when he said you're going to sweat."

He climbed the deck stairs, still talking.

"One last word of advice. We made it clear to your parents that you were not allowed to bring junk food. I'm thinking that *some* of you might have tried to sneak in some snacks. I'm not going to search any bags, but I will say this: Don't drop any crumbs!" He opened the sliding door, stepped into the cottage and gave us one last look. "Out here, the rats are as big as cats, and if they get a taste for treats, they'll come for you in your sleep!" He gave an evil laugh and slid the glass door shut.

Dion squealed, then clapped both hands over his mouth.

Maybe Sensei Rick did understand kids after all.

THIRTEEN

The five of us looked at one another.

Ignoring the bags, we took off as a pack, laughing as we raced from one trailer to the next. At each stop, we jumped over worn wooden steps and ran inside.

There wasn't much difference between them. The first one was pale yellow with faded brown letters on the outside. It smelled musty inside. The next one was pale blue with faded orange letters on the outside. And smelled musty inside. The third trailer was a little smaller than the others, but it had a big wooden deck with an awning. Three mismatched rocking chairs sat in the shade.

I threw myself down into one of the chairs. By this time I had a pretty strong feeling that this trailer would smell musty inside too.

"I call this one!" I said, stamping my foot to make it official. The other kids had run inside and were already coming back out.

"Too small anyway!" shouted Zack. He jumped off the little deck and ran for the next trailer, Dion close on his heels.

Wafaa joined me in the shade, flopping into one of the other rockers. She shrieked as it almost tipped over backward, then laughed. Joe came out slowly. He lifted the front of his T-shirt to wipe the sweat off his face before collapsing into the third chair.

Zack and Dion kept running around. Maybe they thought there was treasure hidden in one of the trailers. They shouted about how awesome it was going to be to finally get their own rooms, even their own *houses*. They went to pick up their bags and argued the whole way there about who would get which trailer. When they came back, they headed for opposite sides of the camp.

"Finally, a break from your snoring!" shouted Zack, heading into the pale-blue trailer.

"Finally, a break from your farting!" Dion shouted back, choosing the trailer closest to the cliff edge. "I can't believe you don't wake yourself up!" He squished his hand against his mouth and made a long rude sound before going inside and slamming his screen door.

Zack's face appeared at his door. He pushed his nose hard against the screen and shouted, "I do *NOT* fart in my sleep!"

A window in Dion's trailer flew open. Dion's head popped out. He didn't say a word. He just pinched his nose and waved his other hand in front of his face.

Zack pulled a lace curtain across his doorway.

Dion slammed his window shut and then pulled his blinds down with a clatter.

The rest of us really enjoyed the silence.

Three glorious seconds of silence.

Dion yelped. He shot out of the trailer, dragging his bag behind him.

"Spider!" he cried as he ran past us. He lifted his bag and pulled the strap over his shoulder. "*Big* spider! *Killer* spider!"

He'd started shouting before he was even halfway to Zack's trailer. "Mama said we have to share a room, you know! I let you pick the trailer, so I get to pick the bed!"

The three of us just rocked in our chairs and laughed.

After a few moments of peace, Joe spoke up. He sounded a little uncomfortable. "You mind if I bunk with you, Riley?" he asked. "I've, uh, never really been on a sleepover before."

"No problem," I said. "Me neither. But only on one condition."

"Really?" Wafaa asked. "You have high standards?"

I gave her a serious look. "As long as he doesn't fart in his sleep."

She burst out laughing. Copying Dion, Joe put his hand on his mouth and ripped a big fart sound.

"Boys are so gross," Wafaa said, still laughing. "*And* total scaredy-cats. I can't believe Dion gave up the only trailer with a lake view because of one little bug. I guess I'll take that one."

Wafaa stood up and wandered over to have a look at her new home. She was in there for just a few moments before she came back out. She only had one sneaker on. The other was balanced carefully in her hand. She gave us a look and put a finger to her lips, then put her hand over her mouth, holding back her giggles.

Wafaa ran across the grass to Zack's—and now Dion's—trailer with a funny hop-step. It was uneven because of her one sock foot. I knew I would never call her a ninja again, but she sure did move as quiet as one. She climbed their stairs and slowly pulled their door open.

The sound of the brothers arguing came out clearly, like two birds chirping. Wafaa reached inside the doorway and turned the sneaker upside down. She gave it a shake, then looked inside it. She turned it over again and knocked it once against the floor.

Then she jumped back and slid the door shut with a bang.

The boys stopped arguing.

Wafaa raced toward the van, pulling her shoe on as she ran. Once she'd picked up her bag, she took her sweet time walking back to her own trailer by the lake.

Just as she reached her door matching screams filled the air, coming from inside the brothers' trailer.

"*SPIDER!*"

"You know," I said to Joe, "I think she's finally starting to like us."

Zack and Dion ran out of their trailer, tripping over each other in their panic.

"Yep," said Joe. He stopped rocking and pointed at the brothers. "But remind me to never get on her bad side." He started rocking again.

I laughed as I stood up to get my bag. "You make a good point, roomie."

FOURTEEN

After Joe and I had unpacked a little, we went over to check out the view from Wafaa's trailer. We ended up spending the next little while chilling out there. Sensei Rick had told us not to bring any electronics, but apparently he'd forgotten to tell the parents this, because Dad had let me pack an old laptop and some DVDs. I raced back to our trailer and grabbed them. Joe had brought his own pillow from home. I was a little jealous. I had thought of doing that, too, but was afraid I'd get teased for looking like a baby. My jealousy disappeared when Joe emptied the pillowcase onto Wafaa's floor. A ton of chocolate bars and candy tumbled out.

"No crumbs!" Wafaa said. "Spiders I can handle. Rats...not so much!"

We loaded up the bed in her spare bedroom with all the pillows from our two trailers. I put on an old movie about a man who takes his three grandsons up to his cottage and teaches them how to kick butt, ninja style. Dad had said it was very *apropos*. Professor talk for "good pick."

We cranked open the bedroom's two small windows. Wafaa plugged in a fan she had found in one of the cupboards. The blades didn't move at first, but the fan came to life when she smacked it. Sweet summer air from outside was finally chasing out the musty smell.

We all settled into our nest in the cool, dark room and enjoyed some secret snacks and tricky ninja moves. Just as the movie ended, we heard two sharp whistle blasts. All three of us jumped.

Wafaa slammed the laptop shut and quickly shoved it under the pillows.

Joe scooped up all the empty candy wrappers.

I ran to the front window to peek out, but the window was small and dirty, so I couldn't see much.

Wafaa and Joe stood behind me, waiting for a report. I looked back at them and shrugged.

The three of us slowly opened the door and wandered out into the afternoon sun. It took a while for my eyes to adjust to the bright light. When they did, I didn't believe what I was seeing.

A dojo.

A dojo had appeared in the middle of the clearing.

I blinked again and rubbed my eyes. Blocked the sun with my hand and checked again.

Yep.

A dojo.

Or, at least, a dojo floor. The whole thing rested on a low wooden stage only a few of inches off the ground. White mats sat edge to edge on top of the wood. Like everything else here, the mats were a little worn. Even from where I stood I could see a couple of patches made from duct tape.

Was the sun making me see things?

If it was a mirage, I was also hallucinating Sensei Rick. He stood beside the dojo floor, swinging a whistle around his finger. In his other hand he held a crumpled sheet of paper. Dion lay on the grass at his feet, fanning himself with another piece of paper. Zack stood at the side, holding an electric screwdriver in his hand. He pointed it at us and pressed the button. *Buzzzzzzz.*

"Nice of you to join us," he said. "Now that all the work is done."

The three of us stared.

"Kondo Sensei's handwriting," Sensei Rick mumbled, studying the sheet. "Sometimes I can't tell if these instructions are in Japanese or English!" He held the paper up and compared it to what they had built. "But I think we did it, boys. What do you think?"

"I think that these lazy jerks just had a good nap in there while we've been working our butts off out here!" Dion said.

Zack swung the screwdriver to point at Dion and buzzed it at him. "You're the one who broke Sensei's fence. It's only fair we do a little work around the place to make up for it." He smiled as sweat rolled down the side of his face. "Besides, we did an awesome job."

Sensei Rick stepped onto the platform. He took a few steps, then bounced up and down to test it. It creaked but held together. He sprang into a forward flip, and his arms pounded the mats as he landed. The stage shook but stayed in one piece. He stood up, satisfied. "Everyone get their uniforms on," he said. "Kondo Sensei will be starting class in five minutes!"

I ran to the trailer to get changed. Joe was just a few seconds behind me. He kept up a monologue the whole time we got dressed. "Finally, a class with Kondo Sensei! Have you seen this guy on YouTube? Riley, he is amazing! He's, like, seventy years old, but there's this one video where two guys come at him, and he gets the one guy's arm, and…"

I ignored him and fumbled with my white belt. I needed to get my butt out the door. Just the thought of being late for a Kondo Sensei class put the metallic taste on my tongue. The Surge was threatening to come. My belt was wrapped around my waist, but my brain blanked when it came time to tie the knot. I stared at the belt ends, holding one in each hand.

How is the left end twice as long as the right? And is the top supposed to go over the bottom, or the bottom over the top?

I closed my eyes and breathed out.

I dropped the belt ends, then untangled the whole thing and pulled it off my waist so it could fall to the floor.

You put this thing on twice a week.

I inhaled deeply like we did at the start and end of every aikido class.

You don't need to think about it.

Just let your fingers do it.

They know what to do.

I breathed in again and held my breath for a count of four. I paused, then exhaled, not counting, just pushing out all the air. I squeezed until my lungs were empty and coughed to squeeze more. My body didn't like it. My shoulders tensed up, and my brain started to panic.

I pushed back at the feeling. A second later my shoulders dropped back down. Maybe it was something about the fresh air, or maybe it was the sunshine, but somehow I had made myself relax.

I took a sweet breath in and stopped thinking about my breathing.

I reached down, picked up the belt and wrapped it around my waist. Then I stopped thinking about the belt. I tuned back in to the sound of Joe's voice and just let my hands do what they knew how to do.

"…and on this *other* video, a guy comes at him with a knife! A *knife*, Riley! I mean, it's a wooden knife, but…"

My hands tugged the knot tight.

I smiled.

Joe shoved past me, jacket flapping wide open and belt trailing behind him like a long tail. His bump sent me flying into the wall.

I was going to complain, but he was already gone.

I pushed myself back up and made my way out of the trailer, taking my time to slide the screen door shut behind me.

FIFTEEN

Kondo Sensei stepped out onto his back deck and slipped his feet into sandals. I could tell from the *clonk, clonk* as he walked on the deck that they were made of wood. He was wearing the heavy white aikido uniform top, plus the swishy black pants of an instructor. However hot we were going to be, he was going to be hotter.

When he reached us, he kicked off his sandals into the grass and hopped onto the platform with a loud *thud*. I felt the whole stage shudder. He sure was solid.

Just like at home, Sensei Rick called for us to line up, kneeling in *seiza*. Unlike at home, he kneeled at the end of our line like any other student. Kondo Sensei took the teacher position, front and center.

"*Mokuso!*" called Sensei Rick. "Close your eyes!"

Sensei Rick's voice was always serious, but today it sounded extra sharp. I wondered if he felt like I did when I sat in front of him. That any little thing he did, if it wasn't perfect, might get him in trouble. Somehow the idea that *he* might be nervous helped me feel more relaxed.

I closed my eyes. The sun was warm on my face. The smell of grass filled my nose. A cool breeze blew across my cheek, and a different smell, maybe the lake, washed past.

"*Mokuso yame!*" barked Sensei Rick. "Open your eyes!"

At home, opening my eyes at the start of class usually brings on the first feelings of the Surge. Pressure in my forehead and a small sick feeling in my gut. It's triggered because I know Sensei Rick is going to push us hard for an hour, and I don't know what that will look or feel like. Each class, I've wished that I had done something, anything, to prepare. I've felt it even though he's never told us what we'll be doing in the next class. One time I asked Sensei Rick if he could tell me what was coming up next time. He didn't even think it over. He was shaking his head no before I'd even finished asking. He said the whole point of aikido is to prepare for the unexpected. To act boldly even when we feel anxious or unsure.

But today when I opened my eyes and saw so much sky and grass and trees all around, I felt a different kind of energy. It was like a mini Surge, but a *good* one. It didn't paralyze me or build pressure in my head. I didn't know what Kondo Sensei was going to be like as a teacher, but I felt more excited than anything. Excited and ready.

The warm-ups were shorter than usual. With the sun beaming down on us, we were already pretty hot. Wafaa wasn't even wearing her padded hijab. Instead, she wore a light one that wrapped up all her hair but left her neck and ears open to the breeze.

When it was time for the technique, Kondo Sensei called up Sensei Rick to be *uke*, the "fall guy." Being so senior, Kondo Sensei would always be *sh'te*, the one doing the technique. He showed us a technique we had practiced at our home dojo many times.

I figured Kondo Sensei didn't know that, though, because he took his time showing it to us. He explained all the steps one by one, as if we had never seen them before. But it wasn't boring. Hearing it in his voice, with his different words for the same moves, made it feel fresh and familiar at the same time. He described each step as he did it.

"Shuffle-strike!

"Turn the elbow ooooo-ver.

"Cut down.

"Uke down on one knee.

"Cross-step one. Knee into armpit—knock him down!

"Cross-step two. Bring up back foot."

Kondo Sensei had struck at Sensei Rick, turned him around, then guided him face down to the mats. He carefully stretched out Sensei Rick's arm as he kneeled down and set up for the final pin.

"Knee. Wrist. Other knee. Hand on elbow.

"Breathe out…

"Aaaand...the pin."

I breathed out in time with Kondo Sensei as he sunk his weight into his partner's elbow. I had played the *uke* role plenty of times, so I knew Sensei Rick was waiting until he couldn't even wiggle his arm. Then he tapped the mat with his free hand. This technique never hurt. But when it was done right, you couldn't get up no matter what you tried.

The two teachers faced each other, kneeling, and bowed. Still kneeling, they turned and bowed to us. "You try!" Kondo Sensei said. *"HAJIME!"*

Sensei Rick grabbed me to be his partner. Working with a teacher made me tense, and that made my moves rough, but Sensei Rick helped smooth them out by cooperating at every step. He didn't complain when I twisted his arm too much, and when I pushed him toward the ground, he glided down without fighting back.

Kondo Sensei walked back and forth along the white mats. When he interrupted to make corrections, he was loud but never annoyed. It was a lot different from Sensei Rick's style.

Soon Kondo Sensei asked us to sit. He called up Sensei Rick to be *uke* as he taught another technique. Again it was one we had done many times before. And again he made it feel fresh. When he asked us to try it, he told us to switch partners. This gave me a turn with Dion.

We didn't work together as smoothly as Sensei Rick and I had, but we had fun getting a little rough.

"*ReLAX!*" Kondo Sensei hollered as he walked by. He was smiling.

At home, I always keep a close eye on the clock. Even though I've gotten a lot more comfortable there, I still know that any class could bring pain or embarrassment, and watching the clock helps me measure my chances of survival.

Here, there was no clock to keep an eye on. We sweated, and we worked the techniques until they worked. Then we sweated some more. Kondo Sensei walked us through two more familiar techniques, telling us to switch partners each time.

Finally Kondo Sensei called us to a halt.

"*YAME!* Back to the line!" Kondo Sensei walked to the front of the mats and knelt down.

"Everybody's working hard, sweating lots! Just remember, learning to fall is even more important than doing the technique. Everybody's banging around, trying to be strong, but *uke* is the more important, not *sh'te*. No matter how many times you go down, you gotta get back up! Fall down seven times, gotta get up eight! That's what you need to make it through!

"Now, go take a shower, get changed, drink *LOTS* of water. In a couple hours we eat." He slapped his belly. "*STEAKS!*" he said. "For me and Ricky. Hot dogs for the kids. Ricky's gonna give you sticks so you can cook on the fire."

Ricky?

My belly shook as I squeezed in my laughter. Soon it was so built up that I had to bite the insides of my cheeks so I wouldn't get busted. I had made it through a whole class without getting yelled at for being silly, and I didn't want to blow it now.

But our big, tough, bossy, always-serious, some-times-mean Sensei Rick...

RICKY?

At the front of the mats, Kondo Sensei bowed from his kneeling position and called out, "*Osu!*"

We returned the bow, and I finally got my giggles under control. "*Osu!*" we replied together.

I straightened up and saw perfect sweaty palm prints where I had touched the mat.

They wouldn't last, but I had made my mark up here.

Kondo Sensei walked to the edge of the platform. He bowed once more standing, then turned and hopped down to the grass. He slipped his sandals on and walked back to the cottage.

"That was epic," said Zack, his face bright pink.

"Well, when you train with the best…" Wafaa said. She brushed imaginary dirt off her shoulder. It sounded like she thought Zack was complimenting *her*. Then she smiled so we knew she was joking. "Seriously, though, Kondo Sensei is unbelievable."

"Summer training overall is pretty special," Sensei Rick said. "Just wait for the midnight moonlight class!" He seemed much more relaxed up here too.

"You're joking!" said Dion. "Are you joking?"

Sensei Rick laughed. "The adults have done it, but I don't think Kondo Sensei would want to disturb your sleep. You guys are going to get pretty tired out as it is."

He bowed at the edge of the mats. "Two hours, guys," he said. "For me, air conditioning and a nap. For you, warm showers and shady decks! Don't be jealous. I spent years in the trailers. I've paid my dues!" He hopped down and walked off.

"For a guy who doesn't want us to be jealous," Zack said, "he sure does mention that air conditioning a lot."

We dragged our sweaty selves off the mats and made our way back to our trailers.

As soon as we were through the door of ours, Joe started ranting about how great Kondo Sensei was.

I agreed. But I was way too tired to say so.

I showered, then pulled on my shorts and T-shirt from before. I noticed that Joe had finally stopped talking. I went to his bedroom doorway and saw that he was sound asleep.

Not a bad idea.

I lay down on my own bed and closed my eyes. Just as I was dozing off, I rolled over and felt a tiny sting, high on the outside of my leg. I sat up fast. I felt a surge of panic, and my mind flashed to Dion and the spider.

I'm so sorry I laughed! I'm so sorry I laughed!

I frantically swiped at my leg with both hands, but when I slowed down to check, I didn't see anything moving, not on my leg, not on the floor.

Very slowly and very, very carefully, I pulled my shorts pocket open as wide as it could go.

I peeked in.

Something folded.

A little staple hanging loose in one corner. One bent end made for a tiny spike sticking out.

I exhaled and closed my eyes. Relief flooded through me. I wasn't going to die from a spider bite!

I pulled out the picture and flopped back onto the bed. Unfolded it.

Mom up in the cherry tree.

I picked out the staple and flicked it across the room.

Another look at the picture. *I miss you so much, Mom.*

I folded it up again and shoved it back into my pocket.

Time to sleep.

SIXTEEN

Knocking woke me.

I sat up like a shot and looked around, unsure where I was. A dark room with fake-wood walls. I blinked a couple of times, and the whole day rushed back to me. My head was feeling fuzzy, but I got up and went to the trailer door. Dion stood outside the screen.

"Hey, dude," I said, stretching as I opened the door for him.

"Rise and shine," he said. "It's suppertime!" He came in and sat down. "I just came from the cottage. Sensei Rick wasn't kidding. They've got it made up there!"

"You mean *Ricky* wasn't kidding," I said, using

my fingers to make sarcastic air quotes. Dion busted up laughing.

"Yeah, Kondo Sensei and Little Ricky! They've got steaks sizzling on a barbecue up there. Plus corn on the cob, a big bowl of potato salad, some kind of grilled vegetables, which is gross but looks kind of awesome…"

"What about us?" I asked.

"Hot dogs!" he sang, swinging and pumping his arms in a happy dance. "So let's get our butts out there. Everybody else is at the fire."

We walked over to the fire pit. It was in between the trailers, just a few feet from the edge of the cliff. It wasn't fancy. Just a big charred area surrounded by stacked bricks. Lawn chairs were set up in a circle around it, but only Joe was sitting. Zack and Wafaa were standing beside Sensei Rick, helping him get the fire going. There was an ax and a stack of logs off to one side. Sensei Rick had set up little sticks in the shape of a perfect little tent. Now he was reaching in with a match, trying to light something tucked inside the tent. It took, and flames licked up the sides of the sticks.

He added a few more, then signaled Zack and Wafaa. They stepped up with scraps of cardboard and fanned at the flames.

In no time the wood caught fire, crackling as it burned. Smoke rose like a ghost but quickly blew off into nothing. Sensei Rick studied the fire. Then, with the same attention to technique that he showed in aikido, he placed a couple of fat logs exactly where he thought they should go. He stood back and brushed off his hands on his jeans. "I just earned my steak!" he said. "I'll go grab your hot dogs." He headed off toward the cottage.

A fire and a cliff. It definitely wasn't the safest place for a pack of kids to be on their own, but that's where the fire pit was set up. I guessed Kondo Sensei wasn't about to burn a new hole in the middle of the camp just because it was our first time here.

We had just settled in our folding chairs when Sensei Rick came back with a fistful of long sticks, a couple of packs of hot dogs and a big cooler on wheels. He put it all down, then reached for a black iron rod that was stuck in the ground beside the fire.

He used it to break up the arrangement of wood he had made so carefully earlier.

The way he knocked the logs down, though, turned out to be just as careful as the way he had set them up. The flames died down and walls of embers opened up for us to roast the food over.

"There's your kitchen!" he said. "Enjoy!" He stuck the rod back in the ground and left us to figure out the rest.

Zack passed around the sticks and we got cooking.

I speared a wiener and found what I figured was a good spot over the coals. I looked up at the sky. The sun was still bright, but it was on its way down.

A long day.

I stood up for a better view. The sun's bright light reflected on row after row of waves. Their long edges danced with sparkles. We could still see everything we were doing with the hot dogs, but before too long, I guessed, the sun was going to sink behind the lake.

Burning meat.

The smell broke through my daydreaming. Too late I pulled my wiener off the coals, where I had accidentally let it rest.

Joe laughed.

I lifted the stick to inspect the damage. I brushed off the wiener and puffed at it, clearing away the white ash. Underneath was one very charred dog.

"That's one way to cook it," Joe said.

"Whatever," I said. I opened up the cooler and pulled out a bag of buns with one hand. "I like them better burned."

Everyone else was too busy with their own food to pay much attention.

There was ketchup and mustard in the cooler, but as soon as I'd assembled my hot dog I shoved it in my mouth without putting anything on it. It was burned, and it was plain, and it was the best dinner I had eaten all year.

Zack and Dion hadn't started cooking yet because they were arguing about the best way to do it.

"You have to poke the stick through the whole thing, the long way," Zack said. "Like a souvlaki!"

"You make everything so complicated," Dion said. He waved off his brother. He held the wiener up in one hand, then stabbed it through the middle. The ends flopped to each side.

The other kids concentrated on their sticks. I took another bite of my hot dog and listened to the crackle of the fire.

Dion's savage approach looked like it was paying off. Everybody else's hot dogs were getting burned at one end, while his was cooking evenly.

Then it started to break in the middle.

"No-no-no-no-no!" he said. He pulled his stick out of the fire and waved his hand back and forth underneath the wiener, unsure which part of it was going to fall off first.

I pulled out a bun and tossed it at him. It bounced off his chest and landed in his lap. He grabbed it and just got it under the wiener as both halves fell free of the stick. They both landed in the bun. Dinner was saved!

I got up to dig out another wiener from the package. There were frosty cans of pop at the bottom of the cooler. A weird mix of flavors in brightly colored cans. Root beer, cream soda, orange soda...I picked them up and started to hand them around. I didn't bother to ask what kind people wanted.

I looked back at the cottage. No doubt the senseis' meal was going to be spectacular, but I wouldn't have changed places with the adults for anything. This was where it was at.

Wafaa must have been thinking the same thing. "This is awesome," she said around a full mouthful of food.

Joe had grape soda in a bright-purple can. He tapped his fingernail on the top a few times to make it sure it didn't explode when he opened it. He cracked it open, and purple foam erupted anyway. He slurped at it. Then he spoke.

"You know how you're a Muslim?" he said to Wafaa. He knew he hadn't said it right and kind of stuttered. "I mean, I know you *know* you're a Muslim. But, I mean, since you're a Muslim, like... don't you *not* eat, like...". He frowned and took a long drink.

After my own ignorance about Wafaa's hijab, I held my breath while I waited to hear what was going to come out of his mouth next.

We all waited.

He looked up and saw everyone staring.

He frowned again and had another sip.

His stalling made it so much worse. I didn't even know what he was building up to, but I had a lump in my throat that I couldn't swallow.

On the other side of the fire, Wafaa giggled.

That broke the tension enough for Joe. He finally got his question out. "I'm just trying to say, aren't you only supposed to eat special foods? Like, not hot dogs?"

The heat of the fire was practically burning my legs, but I sat totally still.

"Well, I don't know about you," she said, "but hot dogs cooked on a fire are pretty special to me. At home my mom just boils them. What does your family do? Do you sit around like cavemen cooking over a fire?"

I knew that wasn't what Joe was getting at. But Wafaa had taken his awkward question and flipped it. I also knew she wasn't really picking on Joe's family. She was just working with what he'd given her. And she'd done it with style.

Like aikido, but with words!

"Don't be a dummy, Joe," said Zack.

"No, what I meant was…" Joe held his can up to his lips, but he didn't drink. He was stalling again. "I meant, like, *religious* food," he said, turning to Zack. "I meant doesn't she only eat certain kinds of foods because of the whole…" He hesitated, then quickly passed his hand over his head a couple of times.

I put my hands over my eyes.

But Wafaa laughed so hard she snorted and then started to choke on a piece of hot dog. She waved her hand and then pounded her chest and swallowed it down.

"Okay." She gulped again. "First of all, I'm not exactly sure what *this* is." She put a goofy look on her face and waved her hand around her head like Joe had done.

"Burn!" Dion said. He pointed at Joe with his roasting stick. "Burned beside the fire!"

Joe crushed his empty pop can and threw it at Dion. He looked embarrassed.

"But if you're trying to ask if Muslims have dietary restrictions, then yes, there's some stuff my family doesn't eat. Like pork. But on the trip form that Sensei Rick sent out to everybody, it asked about dietary restrictions. My parents put down that I don't eat pork, so he made sure to pick up a brand of wieners that I can eat. They're *halal*. Made the right way, and out of beef." She shrugged. "I'm not sure what else to tell you about the eating habits of 'the Wild Wafaa in her natural habitat.'"

She stuffed the last handful of hot dog into her mouth. We were all laughing so hard that Dion almost fell out of his chair.

My belly was starting to ache, but in a good way.

Wafaa got up and threw a piece of wood on the fire. She picked up her square of cardboard and waved at the coals until one part of the log burst into flame.

"Since we're asking rude questions," Dion said suddenly, "why did you leave judo? Is it true that some new girl joined and start kicking your butt?"

Zack frowned and smacked him on the arm with his roasting stick. He had just loaded it with a fresh wiener, though, which flew off and landed in the grass.

"Ow! Quit it!" Dion said. He rubbed his arm. "That's what I heard at school!"

Zack stood up and looked at Dion. I worried for a second that he was going to pound on his little brother, but as he started to step around him, I realized he was just looking for the wiener. It was getting dark, so it took him a second to find it. He spiked his stick back into it.

"You should mind your own business," he said. He sat back down, wiped the dirt from the wiener and stuck it over the fire.

"Yeah, Dion," I said. "Mind your own business."

Secretly, though, I was dying to hear the answer to his question. Wafaa was being a lot more friendly here than she had been in the dojo. When she pranked the brothers with the spider, I'd felt like I caught a glimpse of a whole other side of her.

But that picture on the bulletin board told me there was a judo story we hadn't heard.

Wafaa had turned Joe's question into kind of a joke and still tried to answer it.

But Dion's question had wiped the smile right off her face. She sat back down and started rolling her stick between her hands, making it spin.

Finally she spoke.

"No lie, guys, I was good. I mean really good. And I loved it." She paused for a few seconds. "I probably still love it." She used her roasting stick to poke at a piece of wood.

"So what happened?" asked Joe. He had barely waved a second hot dog over the coals before putting it in a bun. He squirted so much ketchup on it that it was dripping off both ends.

"I was a green belt. And in case all you rookie *white* belts don't know, that's, like, the fourth belt up." She laughed a little as she teased us. "I was a green belt who was even taking out brown belts. Every class. And it's not like aikido, where you and your partner work together all the time to make things work. These kids were *trying* to stay up, and I was putting them *down*! In that exact same dojo room where I do aikido now."

I could see in the evening light that she was blinking hard. She saw me looking and made a big show of waving her arm in front of her face. "Stupid smoke's in my eyes," she said.

She went on with the story. "I was so good that I wasn't really being challenged. So my sensei—my *judo* sensei—convinced me to go for my first big tournament.

"Around that time a new girl joined our club. A mean girl. And I beat her. Very easily." She pointed at Dion. "So whatever *you* heard at school, no 'new girl' was 'kicking my butt.'

"I trained for months. I was so excited. Sensei was so excited. My parents were so excited." She didn't even sound like she was bragging when she added, "And I was going to win."

Then Wafaa stopped talking.

The only sounds were the waves crashing on the shore far below us and the crackles from the fire at our feet.

Wafaa stuck a new wiener on her stick and put it over the coals.

She sipped her pop and stared at the fire.

SEVENTEEN

After what seemed like forever, Wafaa took a deep breath and started speaking again.

"Around that time I started wearing my hijab. Off the mats and on. It wasn't an easy decision, but the time just seemed right.

"Next thing I know, my judo sensei gets this anonymous letter." Wafaa sounded angry now. But her voice was shaky, like mine gets when I'm trying not to cry. "Probably from one of the other parents. They had included a copy of Judo Canada's competition rules. One rule had been highlighted." Wafaa swallowed. She took a deep breath, and her voice wasn't shaky anymore.

"Turns out, there are rules about competing in a hijab." She reached up and ran her hand along the one she was wearing. She patted it. "As in, you're not allowed to. So I made my choice. That was it. No more judo." She shrugged and stared at the flames. I could tell she had stopped paying attention to her hot dog. It had gone crispy black all on one side, but she wasn't even turning it.

Zack reached over with his stick and gently lifted hers away from the coals. He cleared his throat. "Burning," he said. He got up and dropped a few more logs onto the coals. He pulled Sensei Rick's iron rod out of the ground to shove the logs around till it looked like a real fire would get going again.

Wafaa sighed. She brought her hot dog close to her face for inspection.

"Wait a minute!" Joe said. We all looked at him. "So you're saying you quit? Just like *that*?"

I think I knew what he really meant.

I think he meant it couldn't be that simple.

It couldn't be that…*unfair.*

"She didn't quit!" I said. "Weren't you listening?" I kept an eye on Wafaa to make sure I had it right. "Her sensei quit on her when someone pointed out the rules."

I looked across the grassy field to the back deck of the cottage. Kondo Sensei and Sensei Rick were just hanging out, taking it all in.

Sensei Rick could be kind of a bully, and I had only just met Kondo Sensei. But I couldn't imagine either one of them ever quitting on us.

At least Wafaa has real senseis now.

I turned back in my chair and smiled at her.

She looked at me.

Uh-oh. She did not look happy with me.

In fact, she looked like she was going to stand up and stab me with with her roasting stick, burnt wiener and all.

I shrunk in my chair.

I should have known better than to try to defend her.

"*No,*" she said. "My judo sensei did *not* quit on me! He called up Judo Canada and screamed his head off at them. He screamed so much they threatened to take away his accreditation.

"*Then* he threatened to sue them. They said the rule was there for a reason and that some other countries had the same rule, and they weren't going to change it for just one girl."

I knew I was taking a chance, but I had to ask. "Could it have all been just a big misunderstanding?" I said. "I mean, how could that even be allowed?"

Wafaa closed her eyes. She turned her face away from the smoky fire and took a deep breath in. She turned back to us and began to recite from memory:

"*In some sports, accommodation for religious beliefs is easier than in others. By its very nature, Judo is a combative sport which involves throwing, grappling and choking. The head area is aggressively attacked and must be controlled…*"

Another deep breath. She must have memorized pages and pages!

"*There is a potential injury to the hands or fingers of the attacker due to entanglement in the head covering and potential injury to the wearer if the attacker uses the head covering to choke the wearer or control the wearer's head."*

The closer Wafaa got to the end, the faster she spoke.

When she was done she stood up and pretended to do an old-fashioned curtsey. She then flopped back into her chair.

The rest of us sat in silence.

"How did you memorize all of that?" I finally asked.

Wafaa shrugged. "Do you know how many hours I spent reading the rules, looking for a way around? Over? Through? And that's not even all of it. There's more, but it all comes down to the same thing."

"Hold up!" Dion said. He looked furious. "So you can't wear a hijab in case you hurt a *FINGER* when you're trying to *STRANGLE* someone!" He got louder the longer he spoke. "The rules *ACTUALLY SAY* that you might hurt your *FINGER* when you're *AGGRESSIVELY ATTACKING* the head?"

"Or in case you're accidentally choked with your hoodie when they're choking you?" Joe asked. "But...what would that even look like?"

Wafaa looked tired. She nodded. She must have heard it all before. She must have said it all before too. Probably louder than Dion even.

I shook my head. "I still feel like I'm missing something," I said. "You can get a finger caught in a uniform as easily as in a hijab. It's happened to me at aikido. But I've never once got caught in your headgear. It's tight. It's our uniforms that are all floppy."

"Yeah!" Dion said. "And those judo guys have their fingers all taped up anyway! I'm always finding dirty scraps of finger tape they leave behind. Your sensei is a real jerk for going along with that crap."

"He's not a jerk!" Wafaa's voice rose. "You think he didn't say everything you said and more? *He* wanted to hire a lawyer and go to the papers. But I decided that enough was enough. I didn't want to be some, some..." She waved her stick around. She was shouting now. "...some *poster girl*! I just wanted to compete! But if judo didn't want me, I didn't want it! And that's *it*!"

EIGHTEEN

Zack had been quiet through most of the conversation. Now he had something to say.

"But that doesn't make sense," Zack said to Wafaa. "You can't say judo didn't want you. Maybe the people who make the rules were trying to keep you out, but your sensei was trying to keep you in! You just said he wanted to fight for you!"

Wafaa rolled her eyes and shrugged. "It's complicated," she said.

Zack copied her shrug. "No," he argued. "It's simple! You either quit or you don't! And *you* quit! And I don't get that! What happened wasn't fair. But you're no quitter. Was it your parents?" I didn't know what he meant by that.

"What do you mean?" asked Wafaa quietly. I could tell she was getting mad at Zack now.

"They have no right to force you to wear this, this…" He waved his hand at her head. "They have no right to make you give up what you love for some kind of religious…" He ran out of words.

My chest felt tight. I realized I was holding my breath again.

Wafaa studied Zack in the light of the fire. The wind from the lake had picked up, and it made the flames roar higher than they had all night.

She stood up.

She put down her roasting stick and stepped over to him.

Slowly she leaned down in front of him. Her hand reached toward him.

Zack swallowed. His back stiffened against his chair, and he stared at her.

Her face leaned close to his.

Zack looked like he didn't know whether to yell, cry or run. His hands gripped the arms of the chair.

Wafaa's fingers slowly reached for the gold chain that hung around Zack's neck. She pinched it gently, then lifted it. She pulled it until a small gold cross popped out from under Zack's T-shirt and bounced onto his chest. She stopped pulling but didn't let go of the chain.

"Why do your parents *make* you wear this?" she asked.

His body stayed frozen, but he turned his face up to frown at her.

She held her ground. She didn't seem angry anymore, and her calmness made her seem even more powerful.

She waited for an answer.

Finally, Zack blinked.

"Nobody *makes* me wear it," he said defiantly. Wafaa lifted one eyebrow, waiting for him to say more. He tried to explain, but he sounded flustered. "I just...*wear* it. I take it off when I want to take it off, and I put it on when I want to put it on."

The flames flared up again with another gust of wind. A log cracked, then shifted and fell. A dozen sparks exploded upward like tiny fireworks. Just as quickly, they winked out. Wafaa still didn't let go of the chain and still didn't say anything.

"I don't know what you want to hear," Zack said. "It's from my baptism. It represents love." He shrugged and bit his lip. "It's family. It's loyalty."

Wafaa finally dropped the chain and straightened up. But she still kept looking at Zack.

"That's what this is," she said, plucking at the corner of her hijab. "It's family. It's community. It's respect. It's love." She made her way back to her chair, stepping carefully in the dark. "And no one *makes* me wear it. I get a say in how others see me. I put it on when I want it on, and I take it off when I want it off." She pointed at his cross, still hanging outside his shirt. "Why is it any different?"

Zack looked away. He tucked his cross back under his shirt and stared out at the dark in the direction of the lighthouse.

He slapped loudly at his leg. "Stupid mosquitos," he said to no one in particular.

Wafaa picked up her roasting stick.

We sat in silence, looking at the fire.

Suddenly a wiener came flying through the air and slapped Dion's cheek. It bounced into the dirt and rolled to a stop beside the fire bricks.

"Eat up, Dion," Joe said. "You're looking a little skinny after all that training today."

"You...little...!" Dion said. He grabbed the dirty wiener from the ground and whipped it back at Joe, his surprise turning into laughter. Joe flinched but somehow caught it and whipped it right back again. It bounced off Dion's forehead. This time Dion just shrugged, picked it up and wiped it on his pants. He stuck it on his stick and went to work roasting it. "A little Mother Nature never killed anybody," he said.

"*COOK FASTER!*" Kondo Sensei's voice boomed out of the darkness. "We want *DESSERT!*"

We all jumped. Dion fell out of his chair and nearly landed in the fire. We couldn't see the senseis in the dark behind us, but we could hear them both laughing deep belly laughs as they made their way toward us.

"Graham crackers! Chocolate! *MARSH-MALLOWS!*" Kondo Sensei bellowed. As he got closer to the fire we could see him. He held up both hands, each one squeezing a bag of junk food. "*TIME FOR S'MORES!*"

Sensei Rick was carrying two more folding chairs. He imitated his teacher, holding the chairs up and shaking them in the air, laughing.

We shuffled our chairs around to make room for them, bumping into one another, laughing.

I wondered how long they had been there, how much they had heard.

For the rest of the night we stuffed our faces with tasty toasted marshmallows and soft melted chocolate, squished between crunchy graham crackers.

We ate until we thought we'd be sick.

And then we ate some more.

NINETEEN

The next morning two sharp whistle blasts broke through my sleep. This time I was a little quicker figuring out where I was.

That didn't mean I was quick getting up. All the junk food from the night before was slowing me down. I sniffed at my arm. Smoke from last night's fire. And it wasn't just on my skin. My clothes gave the whole room a charred smell.

Another two blasts from the whistle. I rolled out of bed and went to the door.

Sure enough, out in the middle of the clearing was Sensei Rick. He was in shorts and a T-shirt instead of an aikido uniform, so I guessed we weren't starting the day on the mats. From the way he was swinging his arms, though, I figured he had something in mind for us and was eager to get started on it.

I wandered back to the other bedroom, where Joe lay unmoving under his sheet. I slapped him where I guessed his butt would be.

"Rise and shine, cupcake!" I said. I saw a little alarm clock beside the bed. Nine AM! I'd *never* slept past 7:00 AM at home.

Joe still hadn't budged, so I poked him hard in the ribs.

"Ow!" he cried. At least I knew he was alive.

I dragged myself outside wearing the shorts and T-shirt I had brought to wear as pajamas. Dion, Zack and Wafaa had made it outside by then, but they didn't look too happy to be there. I heard Joe thumping along behind me, and I waited for him to catch up.

Once we got there, Sensei Rick announced the plan. "This morning we're going to work on breathing! And the best way to learn about breathing is to practice where there isn't any air!"

We looked at one another. If he thought we were up for solving riddles this early in the day, he was in for a big disappointment.

"Go get your bathing suits on," he said. "We're going down to the lake!"

That woke us up. We cheered and ran back to our trailers to get ready.

"Just one thing, Riley! " Joe called from his room. "What if the water's cold? That isn't some sandy beach down there!"

"So what if it is cold?" I shouted back. "You sweat so much in the dojo, maybe you'll enjoy freezing your butt off for a change!" I dug through my duffel bag for a towel.

I found it and was the first one back out. I noticed that Sensei Rick's shorts didn't look like a bathing suit.

"Are you going to swim in that, Sensei Rick?" I asked.

He laughed. "Do you have any idea how cold that lake is?" he said. "I'm not even going to put my toes in!"

"So why are you making us go in?" I said.

"A few reasons. First, it is a good way to practice your breathing. Breath control is really important in aikido. We count on breath power instead of muscle power. If you practice holding your breath underwater, you won't gas out so quickly on the mats.

"Second," he said, and he lowered his voice a little, "Kondo Sensei and I heard some of what you guys were talking about last night around the fire. Things sounded like they got kind of serious. It didn't seem like anything got out of hand, but... well, that was a tough conversation. Kondo Sensei thought a little swim would be a good way to reset. You know, wash off some of those heavy feelings."

I nodded. They must have been standing behind us longer than we realized. "Makes sense," I said.

"Third," he said, looking at his watch, "it's a lake. It's fun. If we can get there before lunch!"

So Sensei Rick *did* allow his students to have fun, as long it was carefully scheduled.

He gave another blast on the whistle. "Let's go, guys!" he yelled.

"*RICKY!*" Kondo Sensei's voice echoed through the camp. "*STOP THAT WHISTLING!*"

Sensei Rick cringed and started walking toward the wooden fence. He looked so much like a kid in trouble that I had to laugh.

Everybody else caught up to us. We stood a few steps from the fire pit.

"So how exactly do we get down there, Sensei?" Wafaa asked, looking over the fence.

"Easy," Sensei Rick replied. "We take the stairs." He walked along the fence to where it ended, past Wafaa's trailer. He picked up a long stick that had been leaning against the last fence post.

He poked around the bushes until he found what he was looking for. Then he disappeared into them. After a second his head popped back out. "You guys coming?" he asked. He disappeared again.

The five of us ran over to the bushes. Zack just barely beat Wafaa to be at the front of the pack. He hesitated for a second, then pushed his way through.

Wafaa went next. When it was my turn to step through, I was surprised at how quickly the ground dropped off. Two more steps and I'd have been a goner. There was sort of a pathway, but if I didn't want to just roll down the cliff, I'd have to climb carefully down a few wooden steps that were half buried in the dirt.

Plenty of times when I was anxious and the Surge was twisting my stomach in knots or making my hands shake, I felt like I was standing at the edge of a cliff.

Now I actually *was* standing on the edge of a cliff.

It was scary, but not nearly as bad as the Surge.

I tried to concentrate on how Zack, and then Wafaa, picked their way down the steps. Just past the stairs Sensei Rick stood on a flat part. He poked at the ground in front of him with his stick. I could see that the ground was pretty sandy, and in some places the edges just trickled away in a landslide where he poked. I did my best to put my feet exactly where Wafaa had stepped ahead of me.

As we walked, the trail zigzagged back and forth. At a couple of places it was so steep that we took turns grabbing onto the stems of the plants for balance. In other places we slid on our bums to get to the next flat part. Once we had to hold Sensei Rick's hand as he helped us jump over a little gap.

Finally, one last hop straight down and my feet were on rocky ground. I looked back up.

We had started at such a height that I got dizzy just looking there.

"We deserve colored belts just for surviving that trip!" Dion said.

Sensei Rick shook his head. "Coming down is the easy part," he said. "Just wait till we go back up." He stretched his arm out at the lake. "But first, everybody in! The water's never been warmer!" He looked at me and winked.

The waves were sparkling with the morning sun. The water really did look warm. Zack and Dion kicked off their flip-flops and raced ahead, splashing as they tore into the water. A second later they screamed as they realized that Sensei Rick had tricked them. Joe and I looked at each other. I could tell he didn't want to go in any more than I did.

Wafaa was never one to back down though. She adjusted her bathing cap and rushed in after the boys.

Her courage got her into the water, but it couldn't keep her warm. She got knee deep before hugging herself tight and giving a little scream.

She looked back at us and smiled. She was already shivering, but her smile made it look like going in was worth it. She waded in deeper, then dove under. She came up splashing at Zack and Dion.

Joe and I looked at each other again.

I flashed back to our very first night of aikido. Me, terrified. Me, doing nothing while one after the other everyone else "jumped in."

I didn't want to be that kid anymore.

Why should I be the last one "standing against the wall"?

Nobody was keeping me there but me.

"See ya!" I yelled in Joe's face. I tore off my T-shirt and charged into the lake. "Sumo attack! Sumo attack on Zack!"

Like Wafaa, I got knee deep before the water froze me. The cold shot from the tips of my toes to the top of my brain. My mouth fell open, but I pushed through, forcing my way deeper. When I was close enough to the other kids, I launched myself at them.

The splash was huge. I dunked my whole body under.

It was so cold that my eyes nearly popped out. And I think my heart stopped beating for a second. But I forced myself down deeper. I waved my arms and pushed the water up so I could stay close to the bottom.

I held my breath as long as I could take it. When my lungs felt like they were going to burst, I blew out a rush of bubbles and stayed down just a little longer. My lungs were burning, squeezing...

The Surge lit up my brain, but I didn't want to give in.

And then I relaxed. Just for a second, for one perfect moment, I felt calm.

That was all I'd wanted. To beat the Surge.

I shot up, my feet pushing off the bottom, breaking through the water's surface like a whale and sucking in air.

I flopped back into the water. I got my feet under me and stood up to blink and rub the lake out of my eyes. My lungs were still heaving.

I thought back to what Sensei Rick had told me about why we were coming down here this morning. One of the things he had said was that we'd be working on aikido "breath power." I didn't know if mine would get any stronger from one morning of swimming, but I sure did feel like it was a fresh start for me. After the tough talk around the fire the night before, maybe it was a fresh start for all of us aikido kids.

A giant wave blasted over my shoulders and neck, and I heard the other kids laughing.

"Revenge!" Dion shouted.

It was becoming a battle. I turned and saw Wafaa struggling to dunk Zack.

I looked back toward the beach. Joe had made it into the water almost up to his knees. But he didn't look happy about it.

"Joe!" I called.

He frowned. "What?"

"Oh, Joe-oh!" I sang.

"What?" he said. He sounded nervous.

The other kids seemed to know what I was thinking.

"Sumo attack on Joe!" Zack yelled.

"No, guys, c'mon, please…"

Swimming, wading, crawling through the water, the four of us went after him as fast as we could. He couldn't help himself. He started laughing.

"Guys, please! It's too cold!"

He squeezed his eyes shut and pawed at the air, trying to stop the waves we splashed at him. Finally he gave up, roared and smashed into the water with a huge belly flop.

I swam off to the side and stood up, waist deep. I spotted Sensei Rick sitting on a boulder at the bottom of the cliff, keeping an eye on us.

"Is this how the adults train when they come up here, Sensei Rick?" I shouted to him.

Sensei Rick stood and held up a finger like he was going to offer a wise insight.

He didn't say anything at first, so I waited. The sun was warm on my shoulders. After a few seconds he shrugged. He had a goofy look on his face, like he was fighting down a big laugh.

Two sets of hands grabbed my legs under the water and boosted me up. Another pair of hands grabbed onto my shoulders, pulling me back.

The last thing I heard before doing my first breakfall that day was laughter, louder than any of the waves.

TWENTY

My cheek pressed into the soft white mat. From this angle I could see the scuffs on its surface. My eyes closed and my body rested.

Finally, I could relax.

Except for my shoulder, which felt like it was being twisted into a pretzel by Zack.

We had come back from our morning at the beach to find two surprises. The first one was lunch. Kondo Sensei had made us a pile of sub sandwiches. After all the work of our morning swim—and the climb back up the cliff—we just about inhaled the whole stack.

The second surprise was that Kondo Sensei had erected a pop-up tent over the dojo platform to give us shade while we trained. It didn't have walls, just a roof on four legs, so the breeze still blew over us.

Kondo Sensei started right in on the same techniques we had done the day before. We were on the third one, and it was Zack's turn to be *sh'te*, to do the moves on me.

I was face down and loving it. I lifted my free hand in the air as if I was about to tap out. But I held off.

The shade was so cool, and the mats were so soft. I let my hand hang there. Zack eased up on the lock, and I soaked up the break. After a second Zack figured out what I was doing. He snorted, then put the lock back on with a sharp twist.

Eventually it hurt enough for me to slap my hand down in surrender. Zack let my pinned arm flop instead of tucking it carefully against my back. We both sat where we were for a couple of seconds, then dragged ourselves back into *kamae*.

I looked around and saw that Kondo Sensei was watching me. Throughout the class he had been watching *all* of us. Every so often he wrote something down in a notebook. Then he'd keep on drilling us in the same four techniques. Over and over and over.

"Switch partners!"

"*Hajime!*"

"Switch partners!"

"Do it again!"

"Next technique!"

"*Hajime!*"

We were all exhausted. Sensei Rick was training with us again, and even he was taking breaks to stretch out his back when Kondo Sensei wasn't looking. But he had to do the techniques too. Kondo Sensei wanted everyone working all the time, and we needed an even number of *sh'te* and *uke* partners.

Just as I'd get used to one partner's size and speed, Kondo Sensei would call for someone to move down the row, creating a new combination for everyone. It wrecked whatever rhythm my partner and I were starting to figure out, so no matter who I was paired with, switching made the moves feel difficult again.

"Switch partners!"

"*GO!*"

"Next technique!"

"*GO!*"

And again.

And again.

And again.

He didn't interrupt us with corrections. Not even when I chopped the wrong way at Wafaa's head.

I struck at her. She put up a perfect block. Right at the empty air in front of her forehead. Right where my arm was supposed to be.

But my arm wasn't there. It was coming in at an angle to hit the *side* of her head. Luckily, I was so tired that it didn't have much power behind it.

Even so, I felt horrible. Her head got knocked a little sideways, and her face turned red. I guessed she was embarrassed that she had let one get by her. She didn't need to be embarrassed. She had done the right block for that technique. It was me who had messed up. But as Sensei Rick had told us many times, aikido is about training for the unexpected. I had made her look sloppy.

I held back for a second to let it pass.

Wafaa snuck a look at Kondo Sensei as she rubbed the side of her head.

If he had seen, he decided not to make a big deal about it. I saw him writing another note in his book.

Sensei Rick, on the other hand…

"Riley!" he shouted from the other side of the mat. "What was that?"

I looked back at Wafaa. "Just an accident, Sensei."

He stormed over. "How was that an accident? You smacked her on the side of the head! That was supposed to be a front strike!"

I stared at him. "I *know* I hit her on the side of the head! I'm the one who hit her!"

"*Excuse* me?" he said.

Wafaa held her hands up. "It's fine," she said. "I'm fine."

"Sorry, Wafaa," I mumbled.

"Is that the best you can do?" Sensei Rick asked.

I frowned at him. "I said I'm sorry!"

"Can you say it like you mean it? I tell you, Riley, you are just plain lazy! Sometimes I get really fed up with the lack of effort from you!"

Sensei Rick had said this kind of thing to me plenty of times before. Maybe he was right. Maybe I *was* lazy. But this time he was just being unfair.

Something in me snapped.

"What about you?" I shouted right back. "Maybe you should apologize!"

His eyes widened. "For *what*?"

I didn't have an answer. I hadn't thought that far ahead.

"You should apologize…" I stalled, then took a shot. "…for how you talk to me!" I didn't know where I was going with it, but it felt right. "You might be the boss of this class, but you're not the boss of my life! Do you ever think about how the way you talk makes other people feel?"

I was shaking. It was the Surge, but angry. I didn't even talk like this to my parents.

A calm voice came from the corner.

"*Yame.* That's enough for today." Kondo Sensei had risen from where he was kneeling and was making his way to the front of the mats. "Line up."

In the morning I had held my breath under the water and beaten the Surge.

Now I had blown it. I wasn't even mad anymore, but my hands wouldn't stop shaking.

There was nothing to do except to line up, to kneel in *seiza*.

We bowed as usual and called out, "*Osu!*"

But instead of dismissing us right away, Kondo Sensei sat for a minute in silence. When he spoke, it sounded like he was being extra careful with his words.

"Sometimes mistakes happen," he said. "We're working hard here, training lots. Mistakes are gonna happen. Deep down, if you care about what you are doing, lots of feeling can come out. It can come out in different ways for different people.

"But how you control that feeling, that's the most important thing. For everybody." He looked along the line. When he got to the end, his eyes stayed on me for a few agonizing seconds. Then he looked all the way back to the other end, where Sensei Rick was. "We are not karate, not judo. We don't have competitions. The only competition you have is with yourself. Self-defense, but also self-*control*. Victory over your *self*. That's aikido."

He bowed once more and called out, "*Osu!*"

We bowed back and said "*Osu!*" in reply. He stood and walked to the edge of the mats. He hopped off, slipped on his wooden flip-flops and then stood, waiting. Sensei Rick quickly bowed at the edge of the mats and hustled over to Kondo Sensei. The two of them walked off toward the cottage.

With Kondo Sensei's speech, my hands had stopped shaking. But now I felt like I was actually going to throw up.

Yelling at a teacher? What was I thinking?

Was I going to be kicked out?

I tried to put that thought out of my head. But if I *was* asked to leave, I needed to make things right with Wafaa.

I spoke loud enough that the guys could hear too.

"I'm sorry I hit you, Wafaa," I said. "I know it was supposed to be a front strike. I just forgot." I bit my lip. My eyes filled anyway.

I'd hate to end aikido like this.

"It's fine, Riley," she said. "It happens all the time."

"Okay," I said. "But I'm sorry it happened this time."

"It's *fine*," she said. "It didn't even hurt."

"I know," I said. "But I'm sorry."

She exhaled. She sounded annoyed.

"I didn't want to have to do this," she said. She walked over and plopped down, kneeling right in front of me. I had no choice but to look directly at her. I quickly wiped my eyes.

They filled again.

She just looked at me for a second. Then, as fast as lightning, she smacked me upside the head.

Her face broke into a huge smile.

"Now we're even!" she said. She got up and started talking to the other boys about how the rest of class had gone.

I laughed and wiped my eyes with my sleeve.

This time they stayed dry.

TWENTY-ONE

Our dinner that night was going to be the same as the night before. Which was to say, it was going to be perfect.

I had a nap in the afternoon, and when I woke up I looked out the trailer door to see Sensei Rick setting up the wood pieces in the fire pit. I didn't feel like being alone with him, so I read in my room until Joe suggested we go out. By then Zack, Dion and Wafaa were out there, and the flames had burned some of the wood down to coals.

Sensei Rick was a little later bringing down dinner supplies and starting the fire, so it was darker out when we were cooking. We could see the coals turning red-orange when the wind picked

163

up and dimming to red-gray when it died down. The changes made the fire pit look like a living, breathing thing.

But being able to see the hottest coals didn't stop us from burning our hot dogs.

Then again, burning the wieners didn't stop us from eating them.

Too many of them.

"I'm never eating again!" groaned Joe as he swallowed the last bite of his third hot dog.

The other kids talked nonstop, but I didn't say much. I felt like I had said enough for one day. I still didn't know what was going to happen as a result of my outburst. I kept my eyes on the stars. At home, even on a clear night, we could only see a few stars in the sky, and each star looked like its own lonely dot. Here, so many stars came out, and so fast, that it looked crowded.

Not a bad night.

Joe got over being *too* stuffed when Dion remembered the second cooler, just outside the light of the fire. The treasure box. Marshmallows, hard chocolate and graham crackers. Everything we needed for s'mores.

Dion ripped open one of the king-sized chocolate bars and chomped the end off. Still chewing, he ripped open the bag of marshmallows, scattering a bunch of them onto the ground. Joe jumped up and elbowed Dion to try to steal the bag away. Dion hooked into Joe's elbow and dropped all of his weight. Joe managed to stay up, stretching to keep the marshmallows away in his other hand. Zack jumped in and tried to put a wristlock on Joe's marshmallow hand. Joe shook Dion off his arm, then turned and picked up Zack. He tossed him sideways, away from the fire. Zack tripped over Wafaa's legs and landed in her lap. Wafaa shrieked and dumped Zack on the ground. She leaned forward to mash his face in the dirt but lost her balance, tumbling out of her chair and landing right on top of him.

I smiled at the action but didn't join in.

Instead I stood, picked up my can of pop and stepped away to the other side of the fire. While the other kids got themselves untangled and the s'mores sorted out, I walked a couple of steps into the darkness. I leaned against the rough wood fence that overlooked the lake.

I remembered that the rail I was leaning against was probably the same one that the boys had knocked off the day before. I stepped back to have another look. Kondo Sensei must have replaced it when we were swimming.

Was it only yesterday that they knocked it off? Feels like a month ago.

I grabbed the fence and gave it a shake to test it before leaning on it again. Whatever Kondo Sensei had done to it, it was as solid as a stone wall.

The lighthouse in the distance was dark, but it still stood on guard, protecting the ships, maybe protecting us. The sky above me was packed even tighter with stars than it had been a minute earlier. If any more came out, the sky might get too heavy and come crashing down. The moon looked as solid as the rail fence though. Tonight it was full. It was bright and almost painfully white.

Like my uniform on the first night of class.

"There's an old story about the moon on the water," Kondo Sensei said, his voice croaking out of the darkness.

I nearly dropped my drink over the edge. If the fence wasn't so solid, I might have dropped *myself* over the edge. I squinted, trying to make him out. As my eyes adjusted, the shape of him in his untucked plaid shirt took form. He was leaning on the fence, maybe keeping an eye on us or maybe just taking in the night view.

"Not *exactly* a story," he said. "A story to tell an idea. A Zen idea." He held out his drink to point at the water. "The lake is still. Perfectly still. Like a mirror. *Just* like a mirror. Reflects the sky, the trees, the moon, everything." He paused. "Two perfect moons. One up, one down. If you look for a long time, you can't tell the difference. No way in the world." He laughed a little.

He took a sip of his drink, and I joined him, sipping from my pop can.

"Very peaceful. Very *beautiful*. But. One tiny leaf falls down. Just *one*." He shook his head. "Ripples. Ripples everywhere. Across the whole lake. The moon, the trees, everything. Everything is broken up." He paused. "*Shattered*."

He turned to look at me. One eyebrow raised. "How's the moon right now?"

I looked up at the sky. It was beautiful. Perfect.

Then I thought about the story he had just told me. I realized this was a trick question. I pulled my eyes down to the lake, searching for the moon's reflection.

Kondo Sensei watched me for a few seconds, then leaned over and poked my chest with a powerful finger. "How's the moon in *here*, Riley?"

I looked down at my chest. I looked at him. I had no idea what he was talking about.

He laughed and turned back to the lake. "Well, that's just Zen idea. Zen mind. *This* lake"—he lifted his drink to the water as if toasting it—"this lake is never peaceful. Always ripples. Always waves. *That's* real life. Always a ship cutting through, always a storm blowing in. No perfect reflections." He stood up from the fence and shrugged. He started to leave but turned and said one last thing.

"But we can try to make smooth reflections. Calm reflections. Inside."

He looked out at the lake one last time, then walked off toward the cottage. Away from the lake, away from the fire, away from me. I looked back out at the waves. At the imperfect lake.

The reflection of the moon slipped and wobbled. Kondo Sensei was right. It shattered with each little wave. I stared at it, wishing it would hold still, if only for a second.

It wasn't perfect. It never *would* be perfect. It wasn't fair.

The waves washed away at the rocks far beneath me. The sound reminded me how much fun we'd had down there that morning. A smile broke on my face in spite of my heavy heart.

The moon on the lake slipped, then danced its way back along the tips and edges of the waves.

No, the moon on the lake wasn't perfect and never would be. But it sure was something special.

Right then I understood something with my gut, with my heart. I couldn't quite put it into words.

But I knew Kondo Sensei's little story was telling me something big.

And the message was *not* that I was kicked out of aikido.

I smiled at the moon on the water.

Who needs perfect anyway?

TWENTY-TWO

That night I slept heavily. I had listened to Joe's snoring as I drifted off, but not even that chainsaw could keep me awake.

And when I did wake up, it was not, thank goodness, to the blast of a whistle. Instead, there was a knock at the trailer door.

"Hey, guys," Dion called through the screen. "Breakfast on Kondo Sensei's deck. Come quick, or the only thing left will be last night's cold wieners."

Joe and I rolled out of bed and joined Dion in the sun outside. The three of us hiked up to the cottage.

Dion was kidding about the leftover wieners. Cereal, bagels, cheese and fruit were laid out on a long picnic table.

Wafaa's plate was already loaded up, but Sensei Rick and Zack were just digging in.

"Grab a seat, boys," Sensei Rick said. "Get something in you. It's going to be a long day."

I lost my appetite when I saw Sensei Rick. I felt guilty for yelling at him the day before. I knew that wasn't okay. But I couldn't make myself apologize. I'd only been standing up for myself.

I sat at the other end of the table, as far away from him as possible.

"Hey, Riley?" Sensei Rick said. He looked uncomfortable. "Listen...I want to say sorry for how I spoke to you yesterday. It is a teacher's job to correct his students, but I didn't really do that the right way."

I nearly fell off the bench in shock.

He kept talking. "I guess it's like Kondo Sensei said. When you care about what you're doing, sometimes feelings get mixed in there, and not always the way you want them to. And I care about you guys. All of you guys." He cleared his throat, then shoved half a bagel into his mouth.

I was speechless. I had not expected to wake up to this.

One of the other kids kicked me under the table.

"Uh...yeah, Sensei Rick," I said. I could hear my voice giving away how surprised I was. "Me too. I mean, I'm sorry too."

Sensei Rick smiled and nodded. He didn't say anything else, but I saw his shoulders relax as he chewed.

All of sudden I was starving. I grabbed a box of cereal and a bowl.

"Where's Kondo Sensei this morning?" Zack asked.

Sensei Rick took another bite of bagel. "He'll be out in a minute. He doesn't talk to anyone until he's on his second coffee."

I carefully poured milk into my bowl until the cereal floated up to the edge.

A few minutes later the back door slid open and Kondo Sensei stepped out. He had on a fresh plaid shirt and shorts. And a large mug in his hand.

"Ricky!" he said. "No more whistles in the morning!"

Sensei Rick stopped chewing. "But I didn't whistle today, Sensei."

"Exactly!" Kondo Sensei said. "*So* much better! Do you know how bad it is?" He answered himself. "I don't think so!"

He looked around the table. "Everybody eating? Good, good. You're gonna need it!"

"What are we doing today, Sensei?" Wafaa asked. "More swimming? Or are we starting on the mats?"

"No time!" He took a big gulp from his mug. "We're gonna test!"

I looked around the table, and it wasn't just me. The other kids looked confused too.

"Excuse me, Sensei," Zack said. "What are we testing?"

Kondo Sensei's eyebrows shot up. "What? Test you!"

"Test me for what, Sensei?" Zack asked.

"What do you think, black belt? I don't think so!" Kondo Sensei laughed his deep, rolling laugh. "Yellow belt, of course. Seventh *kyu*."

A test?

An aikido test?

For a color belt?

My spoon clanged into my cereal bowl. Everybody looked at me.

"There's a test today?" I asked. "But when are we supposed to study? Wait—what's on the test?" My head was starting to spin. I looked around at everyone. "Like, *today* today?"

"What's the matter?" Kondo Sensei asked. "You don't want to test? No need to worry. You're gonna do fine today."

"Today?" I could hear that I was getting louder, but I couldn't turn down the volume. "*Today* we test?" I looked around at the cottage, the clearing, the trailers. Before this morning, it had all looked so spacious and free. Now it was closing in on me. My eyes stopped at the little dojo platform. I pointed. "Here?"

"Not here," Sensei Rick said. "At the dojo. The Cultural Center."

Kondo Sensei rubbed his head. "Ricky!" he said. "You didn't tell the kids?"

Our silence was his answer.

"Can I call my parents?" Wafaa asked. "My parents always came to my judo tests."

"No problem!" Kondo Sensei said. "All the parents are coming!"

All the parents?

My stomach dropped. But then I took a deep breath. I was pretty sure that not *all* of the parents were coming.

Sensei Rick looked at me. I didn't know if Dad had filled him in on our family situation. Maybe he was just reading the look on my face. Either way, he started explaining, fast.

"The parents were all notified of the test when I told them about the trip. They'll be meeting us at the dojo at noon." He pointed at me. "Yes, Riley, today. Since they had to come to the dojo to pick you up from the trip anyway, Kondo Sensei and I thought it made sense to do the test then."

"Your parents didn't tell any of you either?" Kondo Sensei asked.

Sensei Rick squirmed on the picnic-table bench. "That's also kind of my fault, Sensei," he said. "I asked the parents to keep it a secret." All of us, even Kondo Sensei, looked at him like he had grown a second head. "I thought it would be a fun surprise!" he said. His face was turning red. "I was going to tell you all about it yesterday afternoon, but..." Sensei Rick looked at me, and I remembered our argument. He quickly looked away. "Well, we, uh, all had such a long day that it got away from me." He stared down at his plate.

Sensei Rick was a grown-up, but I realized now that he was a young grown-up. Sometimes he still messed up just like a kid. He certainly looked like one when he was busted.

"Oh, Ricky!" Kondo Sensei said. He shook his head. "No problem. Look, you guys are okay. I've been watching, checking how you're doing. The techniques we did here yesterday, the techniques we did the day before—it's the same techniques you've been doing in the dojo. Ricky made sure you know them. I can *tell* you've been working hard in the dojo. Everybody's gonna be fine." He checked his watch, then looked at Sensei Rick. "What do you think? We leave at ten?"

"Yes, Sensei, ten o'clock sounds great!" Sensei Rick said. He looked relieved. He turned back into a grown-up. "You hear that, guys? Ninety minutes and we're out of here! Just enough time to clean up and pack your bags. Then we'll hit the road!" He clapped his hands, and we scrambled to our trailers.

"This is going to be awesome!" Zack said. "Yellow belt, yeah!" He and Dion high-fived.

"No it isn't! It's going to be awful!" Joe said. "I still get mixed up on when to start with the right foot and when to start with the left!"

"I wish I had more time to prepare," Wafaa said, frowning.

I was still stunned. *Today?*

While we packed our stuff, Joe talked nonstop. "So if *sh'te* strikes when it's a number one *entering* technique, and *uke* strikes when it's a number two *turning* technique, who does what when it isn't a strike at all but a wrist grab? I don't know what you would do, but *I* was thinking…"

I wasn't really listening. I was thinking about what Kondo Sensei had said.

All the parents are coming.

It had really hit me in the gut when I heard those words. I knew he didn't mean *all* the parents.

I knew he didn't mean Mom. But for a split second I'd thought she would be there.

It was stupid. But that's what I thought.

It was stupid. But that's what I wanted.

And not just for the test. I wanted it every night and every day. Whatever I was doing, wherever I was, part of me always wanted my mom to just…be there. The picture of her in my pocket wasn't even close to being good enough. I wanted the real thing.

I knew she would be proud of how I was getting better at dealing with the Surge. Sometimes it still got away from me. Like when I'd yelled at Sensei Rick.

Or like the morning before, when I was swimming. I'd tried holding my breath underwater and I'd panicked. But then I'd made myself calm. I was getting better.

Not perfect.

But better.

A hard knock at the door pulled me out of my daze. Joe didn't even hear it. He kept right on talking.

Wafaa stood outside. She smiled and held something up.

I slid the door open. It was the DVD case with the movie we'd watched on our first afternoon here.

"It must have fallen under my bed when we were scrambling to hide everything," she said.

I looked at the picture on the cover. A blur of green, blue and yellow. Three boys in ninja outfits. Complete with matching ninja masks.

We've come a loooong way since our first night of aikido, I thought.

"Kondo Sensei's right," Wafaa said. "We really are going to be fine, Riley."

"I hope you're right." I took the case and gave her a high five.

"What could go wrong?" she said. "We're ninjas!" She laughed and jogged off.

We finished packing and hauled our bags out to the van. Sensei Rick said that the little dojo stage would stay up all summer, but he asked us to help take down the tent cover. Then we all pitched in to tie huge plastic tarps over the mats to keep them safe and dry.

When it was time to ship out, Sensei Rick asked us to double-check our bags to make sure we had remembered everything. Zack and Dion were missing their swimsuits. That led to an argument about who was supposed to pack them. Sensei Rick made them do Rock-Paper-Scissors to see who had to run back to the trailer. Dion lost. I said I'd run back with him.

When we got close, though, I split off to take one last look at the lake.

The lighthouse still stood where it had stood the day before and probably for a hundred years before that. The birds flew their spirals around it. I could see a tiny ship beyond it. It looked like a toy in the world's biggest bathtub.

Dion slammed his trailer door shut and called out to me. We ran back to the van together.

We all piled in, grabbing the same seats as on the drive up—brothers in the back, me and Joe in the middle, and Wafaa in the front.

Kondo Sensei had his own car and said he would meet us back in town.

Sensei Rick started up the minivan. We rolled through the grass and past the cottage. I looked ahead to the gravel road. I saw the rows of trees on either side, making a loose tunnel with their leafy branches.

Just before we hit the gravel, Sensei Rick slowed the minivan to a crawl.

"I forgot to tell Sensei we're outta here," he said over his shoulder to us. "I'd better let him know."

He rolled down his window.

Wiggled something free from his pocket.

Put his hand to his lips.

He stuck his head out the window and blew two sharp blasts on his whistle.

"*AY, RICKY!*" Kondo Sensei yelled from deep inside his cottage.

Sensei Ricky just laughed and hit the gas. We sped off down the gravel road.

TWENTY-THREE

No one, not even Joe, spoke much on the drive back to the city.

When we pulled into the cracked parking lot of the Cultural Center, it felt like it had taken no time at all to get there.

On aikido nights the parking lot was usually nearly empty. This afternoon it was packed.

My stomach twisted as badly as it had on that first night of aikido class.

"Who the heck are all these people?" Joe asked.

"Yeah, what's going on, Sensei?" Zack asked.

Sensei Rick frowned, but didn't answer.

There were no parking spots left in front of the building, so he drove the van around to the back. There were a couple more cars even back there.

We jumped out of the van and stretched, squinting in the afternoon sunlight. It was bright out, but somehow the city sun didn't have the same warm power as the one at the cottage.

Sensei Rick still hadn't said anything. He opened the trunk for us to grab our stuff. To me, he looked worried.

"I'm just going to pop in, make sure the dojo is clear," he said. "I booked it weeks ago, but there are too many cars here. There could just be a language class going on, or a dance class, or a Buddhist ceremony..." He jogged around to the front of the building.

I hadn't seen Dad's old station wagon out front. If I had, I might have jumped out of the van right then and there to demand he take me home.

What made me ever think aikido was fun?

As I reached for my bag, I caught Wafaa's eye. She had an intense look on her face. She smiled at me but still looked fierce. I smiled back and thanked the heavens above that aikido wasn't competitive, like judo.

I would not want to go up against this girl!

I scanned the group. All of us boys looked pretty nervous, but it was clear Wafaa was in her element.

Of course she is. She's passed a bunch of belt tests in judo. Won all kinds of matches. A yellow-belt test is probably nothing to her. Just another day on the mats.

I took another look at her. I realized I had it wrong. Whatever she had done in the past, I could tell that today, right now, this test meant everything to her.

That fire in her eyes sparked something.

This means something to me too!

This wasn't about dealing with the bullies at school.

This wasn't about getting Dad off my back.

This wasn't about showing Mom that if I could conquer my feelings, she could too.

This was just about me jumping in with both feet. Not because I had to, but because I wanted to. Because I was good enough to. I had earned a shot at this belt, and it was time for me to take it.

I smiled back at Wafaa.

"Get that grin off your face, doofus," Dion said, knocking into me with his shoulder as he walked past. "We've got a test to take."

I grabbed my bag, took a deep breath and, together, the five of us walked through the front door.

TWENTY-FOUR

Inside was chaos.

There were two hallways that led to the dojo room. The longer one led first to the change rooms. The one right in front of us led directly to the dojo.

Parents lined the hallway leading to the dojo.

"I think I'll go this way," said Wafaa, nodding her head toward the change rooms.

"Me too," said Joe. "Might as well get suited up."

"I'm going this way," said Zack. "Try to find out if there's even going to *be* a test."

Dion and I followed him. We squeezed and shoved our way past grown-ups eating snacks, talking on cell phones and drinking takeout coffee.

Finally we made it to the dojo doorway. Zack and I stood shoulder to shoulder. Dion, I guessed, was stuck somewhere behind us.

The dojo room was packed.

Judo kids. I had never seen them before, but it had to be them.

A blur of them. A *zoo* of them. Kids of all shapes and sizes. About half of them wore white uniforms like ours. The other half wore blue ones. Belts of all colors, from white to brown, filled the mats. The kids wearing them were tripping and chucking and choking each other. There were kids way smaller than us, and solid teenagers way bigger than us.

The parents weren't just in the hallway either. They crowded along one wall of the dojo. Even in here, some of them were talking on their cell phones. Others were chirping out advice at their kids. The adults were as loud as the kids on the mats.

My eyes finally landed on someone I recognized.

Sensei Rick was the only one on the mats who wasn't in a uniform. He stood in his T-shirt and jeans, talking to an older man. The other man had a worn-in black belt around his waist.

The judo sensei was taller than Sensei Rick. He jabbed a finger down toward Sensei Rick's chest as he spoke.

I saw Sensei Rick's jaw get tight.

I knew that he knew what to do with that finger if it touched him. Even with his love of pure aikido technique, he had shown us some pretty raw self-defense moves a few times.

One of them happened to be how to take down a bully who was poking you in the chest.

Sensei Rick was holding some kind of binder, but it wouldn't take much for him to drop it and defend himself. I realized that my own hands had bunched into fists.

I had been picked on before. Seeing Sensei Rick get that treatment made me...*mad*.

I thought of all the garbage I had taken from older kids at school. We were supposed to be free from that here.

Even though sometimes Sensei Rick had made me feel picked on in class, today this wasn't about him.

It was about us.

We were totally outnumbered. There must have been fifty of them. A hundred maybe. They didn't stop moving, so they were impossible to count. If there was going to be a fight, we could never win.

But at that moment, I was ready to go down trying.

Someone shoved in behind me. Tried to squeeze past. I bent my knees and used my whole body to shove back.

I turned around to see Dion backpedaling, trying to get his feet under him. He tripped, but luckily his bum thumped down onto the hallway's old wooden bench.

"What the heck, Riley!" he said.

"Sorry," I said. "I thought you were one of *them*."

"Okay, no problem," he said. He flipped his hair to the side and called over to Zack. "What's going on in there?"

Zack turned. "I can't hear everything, but it sounds like even though Sensei Rick booked the dojo, the judo guys figured they could just show up. They have a tournament coming up next weekend."

I had never seen a judo class before. I turned back to watch. The falls they were taking looked like a rougher, faster kind of aikido. The kids grabbed their partners, bounced around for a few steps, then spun and threw them. I could see that, like in aikido, they needed technique to upset the other guy's balance. Unlike aikido, though, these kids were using a lot of muscle when the technique didn't work.

It wasn't for me, but I could see how it might be fun.

Under different circumstances.

"AY, *OSU!*"

Kondo Sensei appeared in the doorway.

"What's going on? Little busy today, eh?" Kondo Sensei dropped his bag at Dion's feet and came over to stand beside me.

I didn't answer him. How could we explain this?

"Oh!" he said, looking around the room. "Judo?" He laughed. "Where's Ricky?"

I pointed into the room.

"Oh, good," he said. "Ricky has it under control. No problem. I'll get changed." He picked up his bag and walked off toward the change room, politely excusing himself as he walked through the wave of parents.

I looked back into the dojo. I didn't know what Kondo Sensei was looking at, because things did not look under control to me. The judo teacher had finished ranting, but he was still standing toe-to-toe with Sensei Rick. And Sensei Rick's jaw was still squeezing in anger.

I leaned in, hoping to hear what came next.

As Sensei Rick pointed his finger at the judo sensei's chest, he happened to glance over at the doorway. Our eyes locked.

He took a deep breath and dropped his hand. He looked down at the binder he was holding. He looked back at me, then opened up the binder, flipped to the page he wanted and pointed to it. He turned his body around so that he and the judo sensei were standing side by side instead.

The judo sensei was much older than Sensei Rick. He scowled and squinted and leaned back as he tried to read what was written. Sensei Rick handed him the binder so he could take a closer look. The judo sensei backed away a little.

After a moment Sensei Rick stood on tiptoes so he could speak directly into the other teacher's ear. Then he dropped back down. His head was up and his back was straight, just like he was always telling us to do when we stood in *kamae*. But his hands were by his sides, and his shoulders and jaw were relaxed.

The judo teacher stared at the binder for a few seconds more. He nodded, took a full step backward and gave Sensei Rick a short, stiff bow.

Sensei Rick returned it.

The judo sensei still had a sour expression on his face, but he waved his arms and called his students to attention.

"All right, guys," he shouted, "wrap it up! We don't want to burn ourselves out right before the tournament!"

For a second the students stood as still as statues. Many of them were frozen mid-technique. Nobody let go of their partner. Then they looked around the room, at the clock, at their teacher, before slowly breaking their grips.

"Time for hot baths, pasta dinners and lots of rest!" shouted the sensei. He made his way toward the doorway, starting off a crowded parade of kids and their bags.

I stepped back into the hallway to give them a clear path. As I did I noticed that Wafaa had changed and come out to stand beside Zack. I tried to walk over to them, but my foot caught a judo kid's bag. I tripped and landed right on Dion where he sat on the bench.

A couple of the judo boys saw and snorted at us as they walked by.

"Yeah, keep walking," said Dion. He struggled to push me off him while trying not to fall off the bench himself.

One of the boys turned and faked a punch at us.

I flinched but stared back at him.

"That's enough, boys," a man said. I looked back and saw a grown-up I didn't know. He was standing behind Zack and Wafaa. I was surprised that a judo parent would stick up for us when we had just kicked them out. "Move it along," he said.

The kid made a nasty face at us but walked on.

A girl with a ponytail and a brown belt came through the dojo door. She was swept along with the crowd of other judo students, but she called over her shoulder, "Hey, Wafaa! Nice to see you!"

I had forgotten that Wafaa knew some of these judo kids. Heck, she *was* one of these judo kids not so long ago.

The idea that she could have been just another kid in this crowd seemed so...wrong.

"Oh, hold up!" said one boy as he came out. He held out both of his arms to stop the line. "Check this out, Madison!" he called back into the dojo. "Hurry! You have got to see this!" He snapped at the other kids around him. "Move! Let Madison through!"

Another girl about our age shoved through. An orange belt in a white uniform. Her hair was piled on top of her head in an elaborate braid. Her face was loaded with makeup, but all the sweat from training had made it smudge everywhere.

"*Oh hi,* Wafaa!" she said. Her voice was so sickly sweet I wanted to puke. "We've *missed* you so *much* in judo. You're a *white* belt again?

Isn't that *adorable*!" She made a sad face like a sulking two-year-old. "*Please* come back? *Pretty* please?" She made her voice even more obnoxious. "We miss your pwetty wittle scarfs!"

There was a word Dad used when something was gross. I mean really, *really* gross. It popped into my head and was the only thing I could think of.

Revolting.

That was this girl.

Revolting.

Zack started forward. I wasn't sure what he was going to do, but Dion must have had some idea. He jumped up off the bench and grabbed his big brother by the shoulders. He pulled him a little, just enough to stop him going forward.

Then he relaxed, keeping one arm wrapped casually around Zack's shoulders. "You going to listen to this troll, guys?" he said. "She's just a nasty little troll. Don't waste your breath on her."

The girl's face turned ugly. Mean. "What-*ever*," she said, tossing her head and prancing off to the change room.

She almost ran right into Kondo Sensei and Joe as they came around the corner. She pulled up short, then huffed and shoved between them.

The boy who had called her over chased after her for a few steps, then stopped. He looked back at his bag on the floor by us. "Madison!" he called. "Wait up!"

He ran back toward us to get the bag. He yanked it off the floor by its strap.

A pair of bright yellow underwear fell out. He froze when he realized what had hit the floor in front of all of us. Then he quickly bent down to snatch it up and stormed away.

None of us said a thing to him.

But he stopped after only a few steps as if we had. He turned and looked past me. He dropped his bag and in one motion yanked the waistband of his underwear around his head. He pulled the loose parts down under his chin and pinched them into a mock hijab.

He made a nasty face. "Lousy little terrorist!" he said.

Time seemed to slow down.

A sound like the ocean filled my ears.

All other sounds around me were buried under layers of distortion and buzzing. Everything was white noise, like being underwater.

Usually in bad situations, I overthink everything. Every little word, every facial expression, every little feeling.

And a lot of the time, my overthinking triggers the Surge. That triggers even more overthinking. And so on and so on and so on.

But right then, I don't think I really thought anything at all.

It's hard to say, because I don't remember it too clearly.

But some part of me must have decided to punch.

Because that's what I did.

Hard.

TWENTY-FIVE

Up at the aikido camp, Kondo Sensei had taught us to throw whippy punches. He'd made us flop our arms around like cooked spaghetti so that our hands were loose. Then we'd snapped them into fists aimed at imaginary attackers.

"Not like karate or boxing," he had said. "Aikido punches distract, disturb and surprise. They break balance. Set up the real technique."

The punch I threw at this kid in the hallway? It was no kind of aikido punch.

I don't even remember getting off the bench. All I remember is that I had the full weight of my body behind my skinny little fist.

The judo kid looked surprised.

And then I kind of went blurry.

But moments after it was all over, some of the aikido kids filled me in.

"It was scary, dude," Dion said. "When you stood up, your face was, like, not even mad. Just no expression at all."

"Then you were running at that guy!" Joe said. "Like you were going to crush him! But—"

"Kondo Sensei flew right in front of you!" interrupted Dion. "I didn't even see him move! He just…got there! From, like, six feet away! It was like the stories about those old guys who started aikido! It was…*supernatural*!"

"It was *awesome*!" Joe said.

I guessed that my hand, instead of smashing into the boy's face, had smacked into Kondo Sensei's open palm.

"You could tell he did *not* expect you to hit that hard," said Dion. "He looked surprised. His hand still kind of bounced off the kid's head."

As Dion described it, the feeling of the crack of my fist in Sensei's palm came into focus.

"And he *definitely* didn't expect the second one!" Joe said.

After my first punch landed in Sensei's hand, my other fist must have followed.

"But Wafaa's dad reached in," said Dion. "He just reached over your shoulder from behind and hooked your arm with his!" Dion acted it out in slow motion. "But man," he said, "you nearly pulled him off his feet. You got some power there, Riley!"

The kid still had the underwear on his head when he turned and ran.

And if something hadn't been holding me back...

Yeah. I remember.

I looked down the hall at Kondo Sensei. He had a serious expression as he spoke with a tall man. It was the man who had told the judo kids to "move it along." I had assumed he was a judo parent. From what Dion had said, though, I guessed he was an aikido dad. Wafaa's dad.

The last of the judo kids had cleared out, but a judo sensei appeared in the dojo doorway with Sensei Rick. It wasn't the tall guy I had seen Sensei Rick talking to before. This one was shorter and wore a red belt.

He looked familiar.

It clicked. He was in the judo picture with Wafaa that I'd seen on the bulletin board. Her old sensei.

"Everything all right out here, guys?" he asked.

Kondo Sensei and Wafaa's dad looked at each other.

"Some of your judo students are still having a little problem with respect," answered Wafaa's dad. "The kind of thing that you and I have spoken about in the past. But it's no big deal."

"No. It is a big deal for sure," said Kondo Sensei. "Maybe something happened before, and maybe you spoke about it before. That's your business. But this is my student now, so it's my business too."

Kondo Sensei's teaching voice was loud. When he was hollering up at the camp, it had filled the whole clearing. But there in the hallway his voice was much more quiet. And somehow even more powerful.

"We're going to have that conversation another time. For now, the kids' testing is what matters," Kondo Sensei said. "But we *are* going to have that conversation."

The judo sensei nodded. "I think that's a very good idea." He gave a short bow, and Kondo Sensei returned it. "I think we have some very important changes to make."

He walked past us toward the change room. Kondo Sensei stepped into the dojo.

TWENTY-SIX

With everything that had gone on, I had lost sight of Wafaa.

But then I found her.

Zack was standing near the entrance to the dojo. I could hear crying just around the corner. Soft, muffled crying.

I rushed over. Zack waved his hand, trying to get me to slow down.

I poked my head around the corner. There, just by the water fountain, was Wafaa, her face buried against a woman's chest.

Her mother.

For a second I didn't even think of Wafaa.

I just wanted *my* mom.

I wanted her to be there.

Then Wafaa took a big sniffling breath, and her mother looked at me. Her head covering was a lot looser than what Wafaa wore in the dojo.

I didn't want to interrupt. But Wafaa's mom motioned for me to come closer.

She smiled. "I won't thank you for trying to protect my daughter," she said. "If you know her at all, you know that she's a strong, stubborn girl. And she's very proud of the fact that she doesn't need anyone to stand up for her." She pushed Wafaa back a little and looked at her, one eyebrow raised. Then she smiled and hugged her close again. "So I'll just say this. I am very happy to know she has friends like all of you to stand *beside* her."

Wafaa grabbed a handful of her mother's shirt and used it to quickly wipe her eyes. She sniffed once and then stood up straight.

She took a deep breath, held it, then let it out. She turned and yanked the loose ends of her white belt tight. She cleared her throat.

"Well, boys," she said. "What do you say we go get some color on these belts? Mine's looking a little too white."

Zack and I put our hands up for Wafaa to give us a high five and then stepped to the side so she could lead us into the dojo.

As I turned, my eye caught the wall of judo photos. I found the picture of Wafaa with her medal and her smile. When I'd first noticed this picture, I had wondered if I would ever see that smile in real life.

I couldn't help her get more medals. We don't have competitions in aikido.

But a smile grew on my face, matching the one in the picture.

If I couldn't get her more medals, she'd just have to settle for getting new friends.

Because that's what we had become. All of us.

Whatever happened in today's test, we were going to stand up for one another. Stand beside one another. We had already done it once today, and now we would do it again. No matter how many times we were put down, we'd keep getting up. Together. As many times as it took.

I was as ready for this test as I was ever going to be.

TWENTY-SEVEN

The test went as planned. After everything else that had happened that day, it almost seemed easy.

Almost.

We needed to wait for Sensei Rick to get changed and for the rest of the aikido parents to make their way to the dojo room.

Dad gave me a thumbs-up and went to sit with the other parents on the floor along the wall.

After a few minutes of stretching, Sensei Rick cleared his throat and called for us to line up in *seiza*.

We did, and Kondo Sensei took his spot, front and center, with a clipboard in his hand. He put it beside him as he knelt in *seiza* too. Sensei Rick called for us to close our eyes, and we did, clearing our minds for a few seconds.

Then he called for us to open our eyes again. We bowed, yelled "*Osu!*" and went to work.

Kondo Sensei called us up one by one, reading our names off his clipboard. He pointed carefully, making sure he assigned us the partners he wanted us with.

I got Dion.

Joe got Sensei Rick.

Wafaa got Zack.

I faced Dion in *kamae*. We looked right into each other's eyes. He almost burst into a huge smile but fought it down until Kondo Sensei yelled, "*Hajime!*"

Then Dion's smile disappeared, and he chopped as hard as he could at my head.

My shoulders relaxed. *I know what to do.*

At times I caught sight of what the other kids were doing as I was doing it. We didn't all do everything exactly right or at exactly the same time.

I told myself that it was okay. That it wasn't a dance recital.

Dion and I held our own as Kondo Sensei kept up the pace.

"Right side! Left side! *Sh'te–uke* change! *Hajime!*"

We went faster than we ever had in training, and both of us started to sweat. The sweat made things slippery. On one technique, my hands shot right off Dion's wrist instead of grabbing it and turning his arm over.

I couldn't help it. I looked up at Kondo Sensei. Of course he was looking right at me.

Breathe.

I inhaled, straightened my posture and took Dion's wrist again. I found my grip and put him down.

I was doing it!

I looked back at Sensei. He had moved on.

Then, just when I felt I was really building up my power, getting into the groove, it was all over.

"*Yame!*" Kondo Sensei called.

We stood in a line. My chest was rising and falling, and I could hear the other kids breathing heavily too. Sweat ran into my eyes, but I didn't move to wipe it away.

Kondo Sensei waved Sensei Rick over and showed him the clipboard. Pointing, frowning, they went back and forth in a hushed conversation. Finally, they both nodded.

Sensei Rick ran back to join us in line, waving us back a step and gesturing for us to kneel in *seiza*.

Kondo Sensei opened his mouth to speak and then paused, considering carefully. Choosing just the right words.

"No problem," he finally said. "Everybody, no problem." He led the applause. The parents joined in. "Even you, Ricky!" Kondo Sensei said. "Congratulations on passing your yellow belt test again! Good *uke*!"

Sensei Rick laughed. "The kids really held their own today, Sensei," he said. "If I looked good as *uke*, it's only because they did a great job of *sh'te*!"

Kondo Sensei smiled. Then he bowed, yelled "*Osu!*" and made his way to the door.

"*Osu!*" we yelled back.

Was that it?

I looked sideways and caught Wafaa's eye.

I was glad to see that even she had worked up a sweat.

She just smiled and shrugged.

"AY, *OSU!*" Kondo Sensei bellowed again from the door. He bowed once more and stepped out into the hall.

"*Osu!*" we yelled again.

The parents rose slowly, looking proud but not quite sure what to do. Then Wafaa's mom started walking over to her daughter. Wafaa's dad followed, smiling from ear to ear. Joe's parents came over too. His dad rubbed Joe's sweaty bald head. Then he laughed and made a big show of wiping his hand off on the shoulder of Joe's uniform. Zack and Dion's mom came over, hugging the boys and speaking in Greek.

Dad jogged over and grabbed me in a huge bear hug, almost knocking me over. He squeezed me tightly, then picked me up and swung me around in a circle.

"*Dad!*" I said. "*Stop it!*"

I was so embarrassed. And I loved every second of it.

He set me down. I looked around. No one was paying any attention to me anyway.

I jumped at him, giving him a bear hug back. I was still pumped from the test. I bent my knees and gritted my teeth and tried to lift him.

It was his turn to be embarrassed.

"Riley! *Riley!*" he said when I got him up off the floor for a second. I kept my grip around his waist after I put him down. I smiled up at him.

"Wow, kid," he said. He sounded really impressed. "You really are growing up." He blinked. "I wish…"

Sadness crossed his face. He quickly blinked it back into a smile. But I had seen it and knew what it meant.

"I know, Dad," I said. "I miss her too."

My dad bit his lip. His eyes filled. "That doesn't mean we're not still a family, Ry. I'm very proud of you. And I love you."

He mashed my face into his chest. I didn't know if it was so I wouldn't see him cry or to stop my own tears.

I straightened up in surprise when the yelling started.

"PIZZA!" Joe hollered. "Piz-za! Piz-za! Piz-za!"

Dion and then Zack joined in the chant. "PIZ-ZA! PIZ-ZA! PIZ-ZA!"

"*AY!*" A giant voice cracked through the room. We looked at the doorway. Kondo Sensei stood there. He was already back in his plaid shirt and shorts and had his scuffed leather bag in his hand. "What's going on?"

No one answered.

"Directions? I don't want to get lost!" He pointed his finger, quickly zigzagging from one of us to the next. He zoomed in on Wafaa's dad. "YOU! I'll follow you! Let's go!"

He turned and bundled off down the hall. As he went, we could hear him chanting.

"Piz-ZA! Piz-ZA! Piz-ZA!"

GLOSSARY

aikido—a form of self-defense that allows people to defend themselves without harming their attackers. The name of this martial art comes from three Japanese words: *ai*, which means "harmony" or "blending"; *ki*, meaning "spirit" or "energy"; and *do*, which means "the way." There are no competitions in aikido.

dojo—a training hall. The word itself means "place of the way." In an aikido or judo dojo, the entire floor is covered with soft mats to allow for safe practice. Martial arts students and guests must behave respectfully when visiting a dojo.

hajime—"begin." A teacher says this when it is time for students to start doing a technique.

kamae—aikido's basic stance. One arm is held straight forward at chest height. The other arm is bent, with the hand held at stomach height. The hands are open, with fingers spread out. One foot is placed in front of the other, each turned out at a forty-five-degree angle. The front knee is bent, and the back leg is straight.

mokuso—"close your eyes." The sensei calls this out to signal the start of meditation at the beginning and end of each class.

mokuso yame—"open your eyes." The sensei calls this out to signal the end of meditation at the beginning and end of each class.

osu—a word often yelled in the dojo to show respect and express enthusiasm. It is heard many times throughout a class.

It sounds like *oos* and is a shortened version of a longer Japanese phrase. (There are many theories about what that longer phrase is.)

seiza—a form of kneeling from traditional Japanese culture. In the dojo, students kneel in seiza to focus their minds and show respect. They kneel this way at the start and end of class, or when a teacher explains a lesson. A student in seiza should be relaxed but alert.

sensei—"one who has gone before." In Japanese martial arts, the term is a title of respect for teachers. Traditionally, the teacher's last name is said before the term (e.g., Kondo Sensei). In English, however, the term is usually said before the teacher's first name (e.g., Sensei Rick).

sh'te—the student who performs the lock, pin or throw on their partner. In aikido, this student is almost always attacked by *uke* before doing the technique. Some styles of aikido use the term *tori* or *nage* for this role.

uke—the student who receives the technique. This student usually attacks *sh'te* with a strike or a grab before being thrown or having a joint lock applied.

yame—"stop." Used by a sensei when they need to explain something or teach something new to students.

Zen—a Japanese philosophy that emphasizes compassion, self-control and respect for others. People who practice Zen focus on mindfulness and meditation.

ACKNOWLEDGMENTS

This book could only have been written with the love and support of my wife, Toula Corr. Thank you for believing in my "second" book, and for believing in me as I wrote it.

Thanks to the whole Corr Clan for sharing your genuine excitement with this experience. It has given my publishing journey a good ol' road trip feel.

Thanks to Michael Ackerman at Wilfrid Laurier University for organizing the Edna Staebler Writer-in-Residence program at Brantford campus year after year. That program gave me the opportunity and the confidence to share my work with an audience. And thanks to Ashley Little, Pasha Malla and Drew Hayden Taylor, the writers who shared their time and attention with me as part of that program.

Thank you to my readers from the old Symposium crew at McMaster University, Daniel Coleman and Wafaa Hasan. It's been a while since the group was together, but your scholarly minds and strong hearts helped to shape the ethics that drive this work.

Much gratitude to my number one reader, Tanya Trafford, my editor at Orca Book Publishers. Your contributions were essential to making this what it is. The insights and advice always felt like a conversation with an old friend. Thanks to designer Teresa Bubela, illustrator Steven Hughes and copyeditor Vivian Sinclair. Your talents turned a story into a book!

Finally, much respect to all of my instructors and fellow students in the global aikido family. Deepest thanks in particular to my teacher, Takeshi Kimeda. Kimeda Sensei (ninth degree black belt) intro- duced Yoshinkan Aikido to North America in 1964. He brought it first to the United States and then to Canada, where he founded Aikido Yoshinkai Canada. Kimeda Sensei still teaches to this day in Hamilton, Ontario. He has taught far too many lessons than could possibly be squeezed into one text, but I have done my best to honor his legacy here.

And a special shout-out to all the kids in the AYC children's class in Hamilton, Ontario, for giving me someone to teach! Train hard with strong spirit and you'll all go far. And if you fall down seven times…well, you know what to do! *Osu!*

JOHN CORR has been thrown, pinned, twisted and turned enough times to earn a third-degree black belt in Yoshinkan Aikido. He also has a PhD in English from McMaster University. He lives in Hamilton, Ontario, with his wife and three sons. *Eight Times Up* is his first novel.